For Poppy Edwards. Your imagination is just the start.

DEMAIN PUBLISHING

Short Sharp Shocks!

Book 0: Dirty Paws - Dean M. Drinkel
Book 1: Patient K - Barbie Wilde
Book 2: The Stranger & The Ribbon – Tim Dry
Book 3: Asylum Of Shadows – Stephanie Ellis
Book 4: Monster Beach – Ritchie Valentine Smith
Book 5: Beasties & Other Stories – Martin Richmond
Book 6: Every Moon Atrocious – Emile-Louis Tomas Jouvet
Book 7: A Monster Met – Liz Tuckwell
Book 8: The Intruders & Other Stories – Jason D. Brawn
Book 9: The Other – David Youngquist
Book 10: Symphony Of Blood – Leah Crowley
Book 11: Shattered – Anthony Watson
Book 12: The Devil's Portion – Benedict J. Jones
Book 13: Cinders Of A Blind Man Who Could See – Kev Harrison
Book 14: Dulce Et Decorum Est – Dan Howarth
Book 15: Blood, Bears & Dolls – Allison Weir
Book 16: The Forest Is Hungry – Chris Stanley
Book 17: The Town That Feared Dusk – Calvin Demmer
Book 18: Night Of The Rider – Alyson Faye
Book 19: Isidora's Pawn – Erik Hofstatter
Book 20: Plain – D.T. Griffith
Book 21: Supermassive Black Mass – Matthew Davis
Book 22: Whispers Of The Sea (& Other Stories) – L. R. Bonehill
Book 23: Magic – Eric Nash
Book 24: The Plague – R.J. Meldrum
Book 25: Candy Corn – Kevin M. Folliard
Book 26: The Elixir – Lee Allen Howard

Book 27: Breaking The Habit – Yolanda Sfetsos
Book 28: Forfeit Tissue – C. C. Adams
Book 29: Crown Of Thorns – Trevor Kennedy
Book 30: The Encampment / Blood Memory – Zachary Ashford
Book 31: Dreams Of Lake Drukka / Exhumation – Mike Thorn
Book 32: Apples / Snail Trails – Russell Smeaton
Book 33: An Invitation To Darkness – Hailey Piper
Book 34: The Necessary Evils & Sick Girl – Dan Weatherer
Book 35: The Couvade – Joanna Koch
Book 36: The Camp Creeper & Other Stories – Dave Jeffery
Book 37: Flaying Sins – Ian Woodhead
Book 38: Hearts & Bones – Theresa Derwin
Book 39: The Unbeliever & The Intruder – Morgan K. Tanner
Book 40: The Coffin Walk – Richard Farren Barber
Book 41: The Straitjacket In The Woods – Kitty R. Kane
Book 42: Heart Of Stone – M. Brandon Robbins
Book 43: Bits – R.A. Busby
Book 44: Last Meal In Osaka & Other Stories – Gary Buller
Book 45: The One That Knows No Fear – Steve Stred
Book 46: The Birthday Girl & Other Stories – Christopher Beck
Book 47: Crowded House & Other Stories - S.J. Budd
Book 48: Hand To Mouth – Deborah Sheldon
Book 49: Moonlight Gunshot Mallet Flame / A Little Death – Alicia Hilton
Book 50: Dark Corners - David Charlesworth

Murder! Mystery! Mayhem!

Maggie Of My Heart – Alyson Faye
The Funeral Birds – Paula R.C. Readman
Cursed – Paul M. Feeney

Beats! Ballads! Blank Verse!

Book 1: Echoes From An Expired Earth – Allen Ashley
Book 2: Grave Goods – Cardinal Cox
Book 3: From Long Ago – Paul Woodward
Book 4: Laws Of Discord – William Clunie

Anthologies

The Darkest Battlefield – Tales Of WW1/Horror

Horror Novellas

House Of Wrax – Raven Dane
A Quiet Apocalypse – Dave Jeffery
And Blood Did Fall – Chad A. Clark

General Fiction

Joe – Terry Grimwood
Finding Jericho – Dave Jeffery

Science Fiction Collections

Vistas – Chris Kelso

Horror Fiction Collections

Distant Frequencies – Frank Duffy
Where We Live – Tim Cooke
Night Voices – Paul Edwards & Frank Duffy

DISTANT FREQUENCIES
BY FRANK DUFFY

First Published 2020

For further information, please visit:

WEB: www.demainpublishing.com
TWITTER: @DemainPubUk
FACEBOOK: Demain Publishing
INSTAGRAM: demainpublishing

ACKNOWLEDGEMENTS

Thank you to Dean M. Drinkel for taking on the book. His enthusiasm for the genre is second to none. I'm not sure where he finds the time to run the Demain Publishing empire considering all his other creative endeavours in the industry. I'm sometimes suspicious his energy is supplied to him by the life energy of former Demain authors. I hope this brief acknowledgement keeps him at bay for now.

Thank you once again to the magnificent Adrian Baldwin for the artwork, which captures the stories in a way both illuminating and unexpected.

Thank you to Blair Erickson and Pamila Payne, whose creative brilliance and endless good humour has been a boon these past three years.

Thank you to my mum, yet to tire of my forays into the genre.

A huge thank you to my wife Angelika, whose enthusiasm as always propels me to write more.

And a shout-out to Mr Mole my dog of sixteen years. Thanks for keeping my feet warm.

CONTENTS

FOREWORD

Exploring The Mind Of Frank Duffy

In our workings in horror together, one of the great pleasures has been experiencing Frank Duffy's mental love affair with horror. Love for the absurdity of life and death. The gripping terror of it all. Pure, existential horror. How merciless and unforgiving our real life can be. The fantasies we invent to try and escape it all. All of it. Life. Death. Our animal instincts carved out by the universe. Do these experiences in our life and death have meaning? Or is it a meaning we prescribe on top of a dark void? This unsettling question is what haunts his stories. It's not just the monsters under our bed, but also our society. A fact we've all become too familiar with. The disturbing fable which opens Frank's book, I won't spoil. But I will reveal it involves religion and pandemic. Themes which have become all too resonant in my corner of the universe. There is the cosmic horror of nothingness. And then the cosmic horror of nothingness and the absurdity of it all on top. In his work Frank has always seen the nightmares ahead. Imagined visions which only become clearer when you reach the final moment of the story's life. The storm clouds on the horizon we try to ignore. It may have something to do with his connection to the grit of life and the grit of death having the same flavor. What are these fever dreams in our lives and nightmares? Who can know the truth lurking underneath our cosmic horror? Where does the signal come from? Who can say. But Frank does his best to take his readers straight to the source. Are we brave enough to look at the sinister face of the author of our own daily horrors? Our own lack of humanity. Enjoy this nightmarish horror escape from the nightmare horror of our real life. Cheers and stay safe out there.

Blair Erickson
Writer / Director – *The Banshee Chapter*
Producer – *The Standbys*

INTRODUCTION

When I was eight years old my mother bought me a Smith Corona typewriter for Christmas. The joke she cracked before learning the reason why a boy my age would make such an odd request, was that by all means I could have a typewriter so long as I didn't want to become a tabloid journalist. I assured her I had no such intentions, and went on to explain, quite seriously as she once described it to me, that if I were to write my own ghost stories it was an essential component in my quest for literary success.

In the 1970s, I attended Corpus Christi junior school in Rainford village. And it was there that I got it into my head I had to become a writer, one who was to dedicate themselves to the art of raising phantoms from their graves.

One of the teachers, Mrs Caldwell, had taken a particular shine to me, this despite my obvious educational failings. She knew I came from a difficult family background, even if none of the other teachers had wanted to acknowledge this. Over the course of one year, she worked hard to bring the best out of me, encouraging me where other teachers had signalled there was nothing but a path already mapped out according to my background.

On Monday mornings after school assembly, Mrs Caldwell had a tradition of reading ghost stories to our class, a special reward for being good pupils, which invariably we made sure we were.

The stories came from a wide variety of authors, but none more so than Walter De La Mare, whose Broomsticks and Other Tales was my own personal favourite. For many months I loved that book more than any other. And then one late rainy October morning Mrs Caldwell opted to finish not with a short story, but with Mare's poem, The Listeners.

That reading became one of most profoundly important moments to happen to me as a child. In fact, it changed the entire course of my life as much as the instructions Mrs Caldwell issued to the class shortly afterwards.

"Go home and write your own short story interpreting the meaning of the poem."

Which I did.

If memory serves me well, I imagined the narrator of the poem to be a ghost lamenting a doomed love. I'm absolutely certain I wasn't the only child in class who came up with this explanation, which probably wasn't that surprising for Mrs Caldwell. No doubt it was a tactic to get children invested in reading, for what could be more exciting than the supernatural?

I've honestly no idea if my story was any good for an eight year old. I only know that whatever Mrs Caldwell said to me afterwards, catapulted me from easily distracted child into one gripped by a passion to write. I suspect she was merely attempting to instil some confidence in me.

I called this collection *Distant Frequencies* because these stories represent the shape and texture of this moment in my life, of a feeling, of a time, of voices calling over distances, obscure frequencies some of us occasionally tune into.

I hope you enjoy it as much as I enjoyed writing the stories.

Frank Duffy
Warsaw
April 2020

The distant frequencies of dead stars still talk to us, only their languages are long ago, almost forgotten by those left behind.

PERMANENT HUNGER

China: Shandong Province

In the life sapping heat, Father Jose rolled a cigarette as a battered water supply truck parked up on the other side of the town square. On a dented side panel Chinese standards proclaimed *acts of sabotage against government vehicles as punishable by death or imprisonment.* At least that's what he thought it read, since his Chinese wasn't much better than his appetite these days.

The driver climbed out of the truck and stood for a moment as though baffled by what he was observing. This was one of the poorest towns in the region. He ground a heel into the dirt as if somehow this would make things more palatable.

On seeing Father Jose, he began walking towards him with exaggerated disinterest, only his eyes gave him away, enquiring of a barefoot, black-eyed child begging for money. An elderly woman hobbled past, a rope wrapped around her waist which was attached to a wooden cart. She pulled it behind her with agonising slowness, dragging her imaginary cargo across the dusty square. The driver pretended to see neither as he approached Father Jose. The priest opened his hand, revealing a thin glass vial whose contents were a swirling smoky black.

The driver gave a slight nod, took the vial and quickly returned to the truck.

Father Jose turned his attention to the weather. The day was getting hotter, the sky bleached of colour, the inhabitants beat down by its insistency.

The driver had climbed up onto the rear end of the vehicle, and was busily unscrewing the nozzle cap on the water tank. He paused a moment, looked over at the priest, and when there was nothing forthcoming, no last minute reprieve, he emptied the vial.

Two minutes later he was navigating his way back out of the square.

Father Jose lit his cigarette, glancing at the livestock cages on the overcrowded pavements. Amongst half starved poultry, maggots squirmed in the gutter, while nearby a beggar was sleeping off the ignominy of his life.

*

Father Jose stood atop the sand dune watching Zhu harness the last of his buffalo pack, the wretched animal panting in the broiling heat. The old man had been working the same patch of land for months now.

Urging the animal on, they both moved with the same dispirited sense of conclusion.

Langoutou village was a squalid huddle of farm buildings and wooden huts, bordered on all sides by the ever shifting desert sands. According to the Chinese Academy of Sciences, recent calculations showed that the desert was moving at a rate of 4.5 kilometres a year. Within a decade the village would disappear under the advancing sands. In just under six years this once fertile valley had succumbed to an arbitrary quirk of nature, the desert transgressing the topographical borders ascribed to it by mapmakers. Most of the grazing pastures were gone, the once grassy hillsides now dunes littered with the skeletons of cattle.

Father Jose focused his binoculars on the Qinrong salt depot, the building canting to one side beneath the weight of a dune. The village children often clambered up onto the roof and would sit there for hours, silent, pensive, staring out at the blazing sky and desolate landscape. What were they looking for? There was nothing to see except the unnatural ocean of the rapidly encroaching desert. Maybe they could sense it, the inevitable looming spectre of their own demise.

He had selected Langoutou because of its location, so perfectly isolated, a ragged, abject place forgotten by the rest of the world. In theory this would make it far more difficult to control *God's Will.* He wondered what the villagers would say if they knew what was about to happen? He suspected they would welcome such an abrupt end, for surely it was better than waiting for the desert sands to drown them out of existence.

*

From the salt depot roof the priest listened to Langoutou village going through its death throes. God's Will had been in the water supply for three days, although the effects had been slow to reveal themselves. Now the human earthquake of transformation was ravaging the inhabitants with sickening speed.

The priest had a rifle with him, a satchel of ammunition over one shoulder. He flicked the safety as someone came out of a doorway. It felt like cheating, but he had his orders.

The villagers stumbled from their makeshift houses, faces raised to the moon as if she could lend them guidance in their new state. Mouths slackened, trembling with a new language. Shambling figures filled sand drenched alleys, tearing at hatches on windows, piling through doorways in confused declaration of their purpose. The priest listened to their eating, his expression a curious unaltered blankness.

Old man Zhu came out of his hut, startled by his neighbour, Miss Liu, who was dragging a goat by its horns through the sand. The old man attempted to persuade her to let go of the goat. The animal kicked against the ground with its back-legs, churning a cloud about its skinny rump. Zhu looked back at the village, something else capturing his attention.

Father Jose swung the binoculars in the direction the old man was staring. Several villagers were walking up an alley towards him. Slowly. The priest returned his attention to Zhu just as Miss Liu rushed towards the old man, teeth bared. Zhu put out a hand to stop her momentum, but he was too late. She bit off the fingers of both his hands, before swallowing them greedily.

Father Jose climbed off the roof and slid down the sand dune into a narrow alley which stank of blood and excrement. The goat shrieked loudly as it ran past.

It took the priest barely ten minutes to light the first fires. They spread quicker than he imagined, leaping from building to building as if they had somewhere else to be this night. Their close proximity to one another guaranteed the fires would destroy everything they came upon. Soon the village spat flames at the moon which rode the sky with indifferent regality.

*

Somewhere in South West England.

Beneath medieval architecture someone in the banquet hall was talking.

"They've done a good job given the size of the thing. As usual the W.H.O. are as much in the dark about this as they are everything else."

There was a tinkling of laughter. Cold amusement. Smug expressions. The priest picked at his plate of venison as billionaire zealots debated *significant impact, stabilization through purity, and a reduced global population.*

A man seated opposite raised his head.

"Wasn't it your idea about the fires, Father?"

"I had a hand in it."

The strategy was simple. The fires would force the infected out of one environment into search of more populace areas, a horrifying but necessary paradox reducing contamination, but also helping spread the manmade virus.

"Containment has been successful with surprisingly little of it making it onto social media," said someone else.

"These days the end of times comes in all sizes," another person joked.

After dinner, Father Jose returned to his hotel and sat on the neat geometry of his bed, before making a phone call he'd been delaying.

"Have you done it yet?" he asked.

"Yes, but you know how much I hate feeding this thing by myself."

*

London, England.

He awoke from a dream that was more a re-enactment, Father Jose having fallen asleep at his desk in the stockroom. Raising his head, a shape lunged at him. She'd escaped, found him, somehow having made her way across the vast complexity of London. Part of him was more afraid than he imagined possible. Another part was grateful that all of this was about to end.

"Father, you were talking in your sleep again."

It was only Mrs Shelton, one of the cleaners he employed. She was awkwardly holding a rain hat in her least arthritic hand, while with the other she tore open the curtains as if to disprove her physical limitations. Tepid daylight streamed into the gloom, warping the security bars on the window. She stood in the hazy illumination, a concerned expression on her face.

"Go to bed, Father."

"I've been."

Mrs Shelton wore the same expression she always carried into the confessional, her admittances absurdly slim in light of what she claimed to have committed.

When she left, Father Jose rang Williams to bring the van. Thirty minutes later, they were driving through an abandoned industrial estate, derelict warehouses sat amongst crumbling tool sheds. They parked up, and got out into a sea of rain which was blowing across dilapidated rooftops.

"Have you got it?" the priest asked.

Williams slide the rear door open and hauled out a large black plastic storage bag. He held it away from him, disgusted to be anywhere near it.

Father Jose had discovered the ex-felon begging for money on a beach in southern California. He remembered their conversation word for word.

"Eight years for manslaughter."

"Are you sorry you did it?"

"I'm sorry I turned the trivial into the unforgivable if that counts."

The two men passed a porter cabin with broken windows and entered a warehouse which once had been used to store car engine parts. It reminded Father Jose of the Langoutou salt depot, a labyrinth of pallets and rotting carpets stacked against sagging walls. There was an altogether different smell other than the decaying materials. The priest shrugged away its meaning, but Williams couldn't help gagging.

"Gets me every time," he said.

Father Jose had first encountered such a smell in a Rio outhouse, a blood saturated backyard awash with body parts, the mutilated corpses of three teenage gang members hung from its walls by way of warning to everyone else.

"Give me the bag," he said.

There was an office at the back of the warehouse, the smell much stronger inside. The place was windowless, the desiccated bodies of dead flies scattered about the floor. Williams pulled out a bandana and covered his face. Father Jose's stomach heaved at the stench. Among the usual relics—an obsolete photocopier, an empty water dispenser, a toppled filing cabinet—a child lay curled up beneath a large conference table. The priest crouched down to see them more clearly.

Dark-rimmed, bloodshot eyes stared at him from the shadows, stark lines delineating livid flesh. He hated his matter-of-fact acceptance, yet it didn't prevent him taking a chunk of meat from the storage bag. He threw it to the child and backed away as they sprang forward, a chain binding their neck to a metal loop in the floor, which snapped taut as it snatched at the food. Williams retreated as the meat disappeared faster than it had appeared.

The priest had found Miss Liu's youngest daughter cowering beneath an engineless Ford truck as the fire had swept through Langoutou village. Nobody knew she was here.

"Go on, you don't have to stay," Father Jose said.

Williams left as the priest reached into the storage bag for another chunk of human flesh.

*

The soup kitchen smelled of freshly baked bread as volunteers arranged tables and chairs for that night's intake off the streets. Once they'd finished they stood implacable in their aprons, listening to Father Jose intone a prayer. The words had a depressing finality to them, not that anybody would notice, not in a place like this.

He gestured at the main doors.

"Let them in," he said.

A mass of disparate people poured into the room, mostly rough sleepers with spiky uncombed hair, teenagers turned runaways, gaunt-faced middle-aged alcoholics, people whose expressions said they were lost, only not in the traditional sense. These people knew exactly where they were and how they'd got here. Such realisation haunted their eyes and made them distrustful of everyone within their vicinity.

Father Jose stood behind a large pail of soup waiting to serve people, his best smile flickering unsteadily. A teenage girl with a faded tear tattooed on her face, eyed him through thick black lashes. All youthful naivety had long since departed her features, her gaze penetrating, sceptical.

"Father," she said.

The priest knew her only as Kelly.

"How's the baby?"

"With foster parents. Best place for her," she replied, before moving up the line for the bread baskets.

When they finished serving, the priest went outside for a cigarette. It was a cold evening, but nights in Langoutou had been much worse.

"Got a ciggie, Father?" a voice asked from the doorway.

It was one of the volunteers, a rake of a man with a swollen nose and chipped yellow teeth. The priest gave him a cigarette and lit it for him. They stood in self-conscious silence for a few minutes, the volunteer looking uncomfortable.

"I heard you worked just about everywhere there is."

"Who told you that?" the priest replied, before realising how he must have sounded. "Is that what they say? Not everywhere, enough places though."

The volunteer flushed with embarrassment.

"I wasn't prying."

"I bet it was Rosie, wasn't it?"

Rosie was the cook, a talkative, cheerful woman in her fifties, whose large flabby cheeks were always aglow, flushed red from a lifetime spent over hobs.

The volunteer laughed.

"Like where?"

"Many places. Only these days I forget which."

"Only bleeding Asia and back."

How apt a description, the priest thought.

*

Half a mile from the soup kitchen a piece of wasteland ran parallel to a disused canal. It was here that the local drunks wandered around carrying plastic carrier bags stuffed with rattling empties, where listless young men bought cheap brown from dealers in cheap cars, and where young teenage girls in tatty school blazers haggled prices with middle-aged fathers from the more respectable parts of the neighbourhood.

Father Jose walked along the canal embankment, measuring the muddy towpath with long determined strides. A man in a red waterproof jacket pissed a yellow stream into the water, singing as he did so.

Further along the towpath, a young woman and a much older man embraced on the steps of a derelict building, anesthetized to the world by their groping. Nearby, empty syringes and broken glass combined in a dazzling tableau in the straggly undergrowth. A figure darted out from behind an abandoned skip. The priest thought of the child shackled in the warehouse office, always hungry, always wanting more.

He entered a street of boarded-up houses as it began to rain. Stagnant water pooled in craters where the pavements had once been, while streetlamps hunched in lines, gaping wire filaments from broken bulbs. A sign hung from a fence: NO ENTRY – CONDEMNED FOR DEMOLITION.

The priest walked into the last house at the end of the street. Its door hung from a single hinge, the wood used to board it up lying in a mildewed heap on the ground. A hallway with sodden walls and ankle deep in litter disappeared into the darkness. Above him, a flight of stairs sailed up into the gloom, some of its steps missing, echoing the fall and splash of water.

The priest climbed the stairs and entered a box room with peeling wallpaper. A window, grimy newspaper pasted into each pane, let in very little daylight. Flies buzzed around his head, feasting on insulation poking out of the walls in intertwined clumps. On the bare floorboards lay a length of plastic sheeting, which he peeled back as if attending to a bedridden relative.

Without warning, the corpse's eyes fluttered open. Father Jose put a hand to his mouth.

The corpse's eyes were gone, black sockets winking. The body shrugged, filthy clothes full of wriggling shapes, hillocks bulging from the sleeves of its ragged pullover. A white pulsating maggot dropped onto the floor.

Father Jose regained his composure as inevitably he always did. He unbuttoned his coat to remove a large knife. One of the corpse's legs stopped below the knee joint, the bone dressed in rotting flesh, exposed to the blade once more.

*

His phone woke him in the early hours of Saturday morning. He reached for it, knowing what the voice on the other end of the line would say.

"It's not containable within the specification of the time frame you and the others gave," the voice said.

"We can adjust."

"Of course, we don't have any choice."

"Estimation?"

"A year at least."

"But…"

"The decision's been made."

The line went dead as did any hope the priest might have been harbouring.

*

Nobody noticed the white transit van as it drove onto the pavement as crowds descended on department stores as if rioting. The priest climbed from the van into the city street, watching people stagger to the underground clutching stuffed shopping bags with naive faith they were somehow safe.

"I don't understand, Father."

Williams was frightened. The priest waved him to the rear of the van. They climbed into the back and closed the doors before anyone could see inside.

"I still don't get what we're doing..." Williams began.

Father Jose took the semi-automatic pistol from his coat and shot the ex-felon in the face. Liu's youngest strained against her chains as brain matter spread across the interior in a spray of blood and bone fragments. Williams slumped down against the doors, his skull a broken crown of jagged shards.

The priest held up a key to show the dead child, hoping for recognition of some kind, anything to deter him from what he was about to do. She wasn't interested, too intent on lapping up the blood running down the floor towards her.

"It's time," Father Jose said.

He unlocked the chain about her neck, aware she was already turning because of his proximity. No sooner had he released her, she sprung into the air and knocked him flat onto his back.

She was powerful, stronger than he'd imagined, surprised she hadn't broken her chains before now. She must have been waiting for him to stop feeding her.

The dead child extended her neck, teeth tearing through his coat. Her head came way, ripping the flesh out of one shoulder. He screamed, but didn't resist, not until she slid off him to eat alone in a corner of the van.

With considerable effort he stood up, swaying towards the back doors. He almost tripped over William's body, but stayed on his feet, fumbling at the door lock, before getting it open. He paused, thinking about all those billionaires in their skyscrapers, deluding themselves into thinking they were exempt from this. Had they really believed he'd lost his faith?

Liu's youngest leapt to her feet, focusing on Father Jose, on his wounded shoulder.

The priest flung the van doors open as the dead child rushed towards him. He jumped out of the way and gave her a little shove as she flew past. She fell into the busy city street, landing face first, spitting dark red blood across the concrete. She rose to her feet, the priest forgotten about for now as she turned her head and surveyed the veritable banquet all around her.

"It's God's Will," Father Jose shouted after her.

It wasn't long before the city was screaming, bleeding into the gutters like the necessary sacrifices they were.

A GREATER HORROR

He felt very little as he walked across the schoolyard the night of the reunion, yet as the taxi pulled away the school loomed, undiminished by the perspective of adulthood. The reunion wasn't the real reason Bolton had flown home, nor was it the countless hours he'd often spent imagining his demise at the hands of yet one more nameless escort, sent by any number of his enemies, real or imagined, which was sometimes the same thing. Arguably, it might have had something to do with the French port authorities finding a truckload of Georgian immigrants suffocated to death in the back of a heavy goods vehicle abandoned in the Calais docklands. For now, he kept telling himself it was because of Atherton's e-mail, even if it was the least likely reason.

"This is a private do," someone said from inside the school entrance.

Cigarette smoke wafted into the cool September air, before Bolton recognised who was speaking.

"Should have guessed, the same sloping forehead, scabbed lips. Richard Moody, swollen into adulthood. Still alive I see. That's a turn-up for the books."

He sensed their hesitation before they even spoke, knew he already had the upper hand.

"What's that supposed to mean?"

Bolton resisted a smile.

"Moody by name, moody by nature. Wasn't that what Mr Edwards called you."

Another man's face appeared, lank greasy hair spread across the skull as if defeated by the face beneath it.

"Of course, Atkins. Still riding Moody's coat-tails, are we? Best place for you I should guess."

"Who are you then?" Atkins stepped forward as if he were the exact same person from decades before.

"I'm here for the reunion, not an identity parade." This wasn't Moscow, so Bolton didn't even dare entertain the thought of identifying himself. Any advancement on who he was would mean reverting to type.

"You're in my way," Bolton said, shouldering his way between the pair of them.

They gasped, but didn't follow, robbed of uncertainty, their legacy rubbed out in a matter of minutes.

In the school foyer, crepe ribbons strangled the overhead fluorescents, while sagging cardboard taped to the wall announced *De La Salle Twenty-Fifth Year Reunion - Welcome - Class of 1985*. There was a table by the assembly hall doors, behind which a man with a familiar lopsided grin was giving out nametags to new arrivals.

"My God, I didn't think you'd make it," the man exclaimed.

"Good to see you, Ian. How are you?" Bolton gave a practiced smile.

"Me, not bad, pal, not bad at all." Ian swept a hand across the smooth dome of his head as if searching for the remnants of his hair. "Recognise anybody apart from yours truly?"

Names escaped the faces he could see.

"It'll come back to me," he said with his usual diplomacy.

"Got to be honest, if you think I've changed, wait till you get into the assembly hall."

Bolton gave an expression rehearsed so often he was afraid it might stick out of overuse. He indicated the nametags.

"One of those for me?"

"Sure, wait a sec." Ian rummaged through the pile, picked one out. "I heard you were abroad, something to do with merchant banking."

Bolton adopted the expression he used when meetings in boardrooms passed into perpetual repetition.

"Something like that."

"Listen, when I'm done here, let's get a couple of beers. Pass judgment on everyone we couldn't stand."

"Sounds good to me, although that might take the better part of the evening."

They shook hands, a meaningless politeness to him.

In the assembly hall, former pupils collided into one another as a cacophony of 80s pop music blasted out. The men seemed exasperated by their efforts, ruddy complexions drenched in sweat, trying to impress their wives and girlfriends. There was an anxiety about them as if they were awaiting serious commentary, perhaps a pronouncement on their artistry. Large middle-aged people dancing in accidental manoeuvres, only for tonight they were at least champions of their own fantasies.

"Nice to see you."

Bolton smiled at a man with gelled back hair and an emerging paunch who looked like every other man in the room.

"You too," he chimed back.

The school stage looked exactly as he remembered it. Tonight a DJ dominated the space, a luminous assortment of decks arranged like futuristic surgical equipment. Someone was hovering in the wings, a dramatic abnormality dressed in black except for the dog collar ringing the scrawny neck. An elderly De La Salle brother, one who was busy peering onto the dance floor as if searching for a disobedient pupil, only decades on. Who on earth had thought it a good idea inviting this man to a school reunion?

In the days when Bolton had been a pupil at the school, the De La Salle order had meted out canings for the slightest infractions. The other teachers, the ones the pupils had referred to as the *defrocked lot*, had been bad enough, but none compared to the De La Salle brothers. The one hiding behind the DJ exited the stage as if a character in a school play, their gown trailing after him.

Bolton walked onto the assembly hall floor, people turning to greet him with happy expressions, until his own hypnotic blankness flattened theirs with a noncommittal to consider any potential questions.

Thirty minutes later, there was still no sign of William Atherton or Tim Hayley. Bolton had expected to find them waiting for him by the entrance. Such disappointments were infrequent these days, he wasn't used to it.

A stranger lurched up to him, spilling lager from a plastic pint glass at his feet.

"Nathan Bolton, right?"

"Dominic" he corrected.

"Weren't we together in Miss Shaw's class?"

"Were we?"

"Paul Johnson," the man said.

Bolton suppressed the urge to shrug as if he were fifteen again, his emotions decimated by the indifference of that awful age.

"Odd Job Johnson on account of my well praised girth."

The man patted his stomach with what Bolton took to be amiable pride. If Johnson had been an international dignitary with a view to purchasing a tract of unsoiled land in the Caucus territories, and not a disregarded face from a previous incarnation, Bolton might have cared.

"I'm married with two kids, both girls. Lucy's in Dublin studying literature. Loves it over there. Susie's in secondary school, sight better than this place." He continued to drone, fidgeting with his tie to let in some imaginary air.

"That's nice."

"What about you, Nathan?"

"Dominic."

"Sorry, again. Married, children?"

Should he say the idea of marriage was offensive, even more so when kids were factored in?

"None that I know of."

Johnson laughed, unsure if Bolton was kidding.

"Divorced?" he persisted.

Bolton spotted Atherton entering the assembly hall. "Let's continue this ever pleasant meander down memory lane some other time," he said.

Atherton had the obligatory fuller face typical of middle age.

"Shall we go somewhere to talk?" Bolton asked, grabbing him by the elbow and steering him towards the doors. Atherton shook his hand off.

"Take it easy."

"I'll take it easy when you explain the e-mail."

"That's why I'm here."

They went out of the assembly hall, through the foyer and into the staff car park.

"Now you tell me why I had to fly thousands of miles for this shambles?"

"Have you seen Hayley yet?"

"Isn't he with you?"

"I phoned him just before I set off."

"Then he must be in there somewhere. Ring him."

"I did. He's not answering."

Bolton stared.

"How did you know where to contact me?"

"Lee Hill."

"Who?"

"The bloke who organised all this."

"Go on. I'm listening."

Atherton was nervous, trying not to show it.

"Hayley got in touch about two months ago, around the same time the reunion invitations were being sent out to everyone. I suppose it must be that which started it."

"And?"

"At first he seemed okay, chatting away about work and stuff, people we used to know, that kind of thing. You know what it's like."

Bolton shook his head, not only to demonstrate his disinterest in other people's excuses, but because he hadn't spoken to anybody from his school days since the last day of term.

"It was when I was asking about his family he got all worked up. Crying and everything. I felt really bad for the guy."

"That was when he mentioned Galway?"

"Yes."

"Somebody else knows?"

"I don't think so."

"You know or you don't? Which is it?"

"I'm pretty sure he hasn't told anybody else."

"Not even his wife?"

"Especially not her."

"Meaning what?"

"His teenage son drowned two months ago. And he thinks it's because of him, because of Peter."

"Are you fucking kidding me?"

"His son drowned."

"And what? He believes he's somehow responsible for his death because of Galway?"

Atherton glanced over his shoulder at the school, wishing he was somewhere else. Bolton thought about describing how he'd once thrown a seventeen year old Moscow street dealer thrown from the top of a high rise tower block, just so he could watch Atherton's reaction.

"He needs to man up."

"That's hardly something he's going to respond to."

"And putting the three of us in prison, that'll work, will it?"

Atherton pulled at the shirtsleeves beneath his jacket.

"If Hayley is so shook up about this, what're we doing here of all places?"

"I've no idea. I just agreed so long as he didn't go to the police. It was the only way to get him to meet us."

"So where is he then?"

"He originally said the foyer. I tried ringing him several times, but he isn't picking up."

"He isn't in the assembly hall, I already looked."

"Maybe you didn't recognise him."

"He can't have changed that much."

"It was quarter of a century ago."

Bolton was about to question the validity of the statement, when the ringing of Atherton's phone solved their problem.

"It's him. Message notification." Atherton held up his phone so Bolton could read the screen *Meet me in the PE hall*.

"Tell him to get out here now."

Atherton dialled Hayley's number, waited, shook his head.

"He's not picking up. Could be he's paranoid somebody will overhear us."

"Then he should have chosen somewhere a bit more discreet than the one place anyone with a brain would have avoided. Just about everybody who knew Galway is here tonight."

Atherton looked back at the school.

"Do you remember the way to the PE hall?"

"Is that meant to be a joke?"

"Doesn't any of this worry you?"

Bolton almost laughed.

"I'll tell you later when I've had time to give a fuck."

They walked through the staff car park, before stopping at a flight of concrete steps. At the top was the staff entrance.

"This better not take too long," Bolton complained, putting a hand on the doorknob.

Inside the reception area an empty fish-tank stood under a portrait of a man in flowing black gowns.

"I don't remember this place?" Atherton said.

"I guess you weren't one of the lunch ticket kids?"

"I was packed lunches."

"I'm sure you were."

Bolton indicated a set of doors ahead of them, frosted glass panels, the words SCHOOL SECRETARY stencilled on the windows.

"That's where us poor social benefits kids had to wait to get our forty-five pence worth of shit canteen food. Chips and a cream bun. Nutritional stuff, I'm sure you'll agree."

Passing the secretary's office was a corridor illuminated by chest high wall lights, giving everything a sombre glow, creating shadows where there should have been none. Damp oblong patches stained the paintwork.

"Thank God they're pulling this monstrosity down," Atherton declared.

"They are?"

"It's the only reason they allowing us to have the reunion here. Get some money out of us before they bulldoze the whole lot, that's why."

Bolton had no interest in these people because he'd felt nothing about them even when attending school. Yet the idea the building would soon cease to exist made him uneasy. It was just three floors of architectural mediocrity, but once it was gone this part of his life would cease to have a reference point. A crucifix dangled from a wall, Jesus in supplication or agony, Bolton couldn't decide.

They rounded the next corner as a shadow flung itself through an open doorway. They looked inside at an altar draped in a purple sacrament cloth, on which stood incense candles in bronze holders. There was a rustling of clothes and voices. Bolton imagined garments shuffled down over bowed heads, dropped onto shoulders, a familiar rite of dressing from his school days.

"I saw one of that lot earlier on."

"Who?"

"One of the brothers."

Atherton looked confused.

"The De La Salle Order."

"Here, tonight?"

"Exactly what was I thinking."

Bolton squinted into the chapel one last time, before hurrying after Atherton with the urgency of the pupil he'd never been.

*

The changing rooms had a stale unwashed smell. The lockers were long gone, as were the wooden benches. There was a click, the fluorescent lights popping, a chain reaction of dying bulbs.

"It's all right, I can see it now," Atherton said locating the PE hall entrance. He moved through the changing rooms as if somebody was waiting to jump out. Having located the door, he muttered his frustration. "It's locked."

"We'll have to go through the swimming pool," Bolton said matter-of-factly, more so since he could sense Atherton's growing unease.

"Maybe there's some other way round?"

"There isn't, and you know it."

They walked through the shower rooms, walls gleaming blackly, Bolton glad the lights didn't work.

He remembered the embarrassment of puberty, when changing in public had meant furtively inspecting the maturity of his neighbours with both suspicion and worry about his own physical growth.

"Almost there," Atherton's voice echoed more loudly than Bolton was expecting.

A rectangle of light appeared as the door scraped across the floor and revealed the viewing balcony above the swimming pool. Circles of light reflected on the water's surface like melted ice-caps. Bolton smelled chlorine, that familiar chemical sting.

"They didn't drain it?" Atherton said, leaning over the balcony.

Bolton led the way downstairs, before letting Atherton step past him into the open doorway of the PE hall. A tiny speck of light shone from inside.

"Tim, come on, mate." Atherton said, shoes squeaking on the wooden floor. His mouth made diminutive shapes, as if reciting a chain of complex instructions in the hope repetition would reveal his friend.

Bolton followed, convinced he discerned a reply struggling against distance or something else. Something muffling his voice. His face even.

"Hayley, we haven't got all night," he said.

He could see very little even with the lights from the swimming pool providing illumination. He brushed against a climbing rope suspended from the ceiling, which swung faster than his momentum should have caused it to.

"Stop pissing about," Bolton yelled.

Atherton bent down, reaching for the light.

"It's a phone," he reported back.

Darkness blossomed within the existing darkness, swallowing Atherton. His footsteps rang out, a restless tap dance played out on the hard wooden floor. Something dropped from one of the climbing ropes and landed behind Bolton. Across the hall, a stifled urgency of noise, a shuffling resistance.

Bolton turned for the doorway, frozen into remembrance as a De La Salle brother came walking towards him.

The face staring at him through the dark was oval shaped, a floating moon of decay. A rotten tooth tumbled out of its mouth and clattered into the floor. Bolton didn't scream, for it would mean dishonouring the education granted him by his adoptive Moscow, a city whose beauty and violence had succoured him according to its intemperate moods.

From somewhere behind him came the unmistakable swish of gowns travelling across the floor.

He turned as a second figure was creeping up on him. Bolton punched the face leering towards him. The brother slammed into a wall and split open, a flood of putrefaction escaping, decomposing organs slopping between shrivelling fingers.

Bolton ran out of the gymnasium and up the stairs to the viewing balcony, bounding up the steps. When he reached the top, he looked down and saw a body floating in the swimming pool, a pink hazy corolla outlining the skull.

Peter Galway.

Bolton hesitated for a fraction of a second, no more than anyone sane would have done given the circumstances. It was enough to allow them to catch up with him, and as he was about to sprint away, somebody struck him from behind, sending him swimming into a blackness that wasn't entirely unwanted.

*

He awoke at the side of the swimming pool. In the deep end, Peter Galway, unhindered by the constraints of death, was tunnelling lengths back and forth through the water, his skull a ripe cerise wound. The brothers forced Bolton to his feet as Galway finished this grotesque imitation of his long ago school life and climbed from the pool. His pale skinny body dripped water. One of the brothers threw his gown around the boy, Galway's face visible above the crook of one arm.

He leapt forward, hands reaching around Bolton's head, pulling him forward, bringing his face down to his level. The brothers added even more pressure, wrenching Bolton's mouth open with decomposing fingers.

Galway forced his tongue inside, Bolton feeling it bulge against his tonsils. It wriggled around, depositing dank tasting saliva. Bolton gagged, struggling to break free.

Finally, they let him go, watching as he collapsed, dry heaving the taste out of his mouth. When he straightened up, he stared into Galway's eyes.

"Is that it?" he asked, wiping his mouth. He spat onto the floor.

"I didn't kill you. And your proclivities meant nothing to me then, nor do they now."

Galway pressed his hands against his stomach as his abdomen tore open with the soft fragility of sodden newspaper. Bolton felt no sympathy, just as he'd felt nothing for the Georgian immigrants snuffed out in the course of one oxygen starved night on a nameless European motorway.

"It was an accident," he said.

Decades earlier he'd arrived early for swimming practice only to find Atherton and Hayley stood over Galway's lifeless body. Hayley had claimed Galway had *touched him up*, only he'd never intended to hit him so hard in retalliation. It had been Bolton's idea to make it look as if Galway had fractured his skull while diving into the pool. Only after the coroner's report did they learn Galway had in fact died from accidental drowning.

"Nothing accidental about it at all," he said.

Galway fell to his knees.

Afterwards, Atherton and Haley claimed they'd no idea Galway was alive when they'd tossed his body into the swimming pool. Even now Bolton wasn't sure he believed them. As for himself, hadn't he glimpsed a twitching eyelid as the body sank below the water, a string of air bubbles breaking the surface?

Galway clutched his stomach, indescribable chunks beyond their original biology squirming between his fingers. One the brothers ran at Bolton, who raised a leg in defence. The brother tripped and flew into the deep end of the swimming pool, sinking amid the tatters of his gown, a bedraggled dying black moth.

"You're next," he said, shoving Galway into the water, who disappeared into the murk of his own putrefaction.

The other brothers, their faces hanging from the framework of their skulls, simply stared at the remains of the bodies in the swimming pool. One of them pointed at the gown floating in the water, drifting by the side of the pool.

Bolton understood without asking, retrieving the gown, slipping it over his head, wet slopping sleeves gliding down the length of his arms.

"A perfect fit," he said.

APPEARANCES

The taxi took Jack through the town the long way, just as he'd requested. Snow draped buildings, bedraggled figures lopping through nondescript streets, an unimpressive grey conformity everywhere he stared. The town radiated misery, and had all the appeal of a leper colony, appropriate considering he was a temporary exile.

The taxi let him out as his destination, suitcase at his feet, mummified dog shit everywhere. There was an off-license on the opposite side of the street, extricating emotions he otherwise thought banished. He worked his way through a long line of self-imposed excuses. Even from this distance, through the sluggish yellow light of its windows, he imagined scanning shelves for something expensive, something with a fancy label, anything to obscure the repetition of his thoughts. It had been eight weeks since the Christmas staff party. Gnawing off a couple of fingers to soften the interminable frustration, was a pleasanter alternative than undergoing a process he wasn't sure he could manage.

Two dishevelled men came out of the off-license, a bell proclaiming their departure.

To a high performance drunk like himself it was a holy sound. The men disappeared round the corner of the building to find somewhere secret to drink. Two months sobriety wasn't much, but for Jack it was a miracle comparable to Lazarus announcing his comeback.

He thought about ringing Sylvia, maybe going back home and looking her in the eye without mumbling apologies. Too late for that. This is your penance, or no doubt how her father sees things. The old bastard.

Jack checked the address to be sure this was the right place. The largest of five tower blocks, forty-nine reared above him; slate grey walls, rusting satellite dishes. He heard Sylvia's father's voice intoning across the vastness of the boardroom: *"you can forget a hotel, not until you close the deal. Understood? Maybe then you'll realise how close you came to losing your job, and not to mention my daughter."*

The lift climbed to the eleventh floor, corridors sinking past, a stagnant gloom permeating everything. A single strip light buzzed as he walked past several doors. There were none of the usual noises, dogs sniffing restlessly at people in the corridor, music blaring, raised voices always on the cusp of full-blown arguments. He inserted the key and entered the flat, where a restless, unfamiliar silence was waiting for him.

*

After ringing the contractors to confirm the meeting, he fixed dinner from supplies left in the kitchen as arranged by Paulina his secretary. He sat at a table by the window, peering out at the blocks opposite his, close enough to see people vacillating between rooms as if uncertain of where they belonged.

He had a post meal cigarette on the balcony, dusk peeling back the horizon to reveal the first discouraging traces of darkness. In the street directly below, a drunken couple swayed across the pavement. Stumbling to a halt, they embraced each other, snow blowing past as if they had been wielded together. He watched them pull apart, heading for a green neon sign flashing into the night. One word pulsated up at him. BAR. Jack was in the shower and a new set of clothes before the condensation had dried on the bathroom mirror.

*

There was a sizeable crowd in the bar, mostly middle-aged men gathered about several large pool tables, stroking nicotine stained moustaches with ponderous exaggeration. A set of cheap plastic tables arranged in no discernible order gave the bar a sense of authentic indifference.

"It's been like this for days," said the barman.

A hairless skull moved under dim lights, while large callused hands gripped a pump handle, their nails unusually long and yellow.

"Must be the weather," Jack replied.

He sat on a high stool and ordered Lech.

"You visiting?" the barman asked.

Jack shrugged out of his coat, putting it on the stool next to him.

"That obvious?"

The barman pointed to Jack's cashmere coat.

"Not many round here could afford something like that."

Jack resisted the urge to be polite in case he came off sounding patronising.

"I've only been here six months and I'll tell you this, these poor bastards haven't much of anything, except when it comes to drinking. Mind you, I'd be out of business if it wasn't for them."

The barman laughed, teeth flashing an unnatural brilliance, which were at odds compared to the colour of his fingernails.

"Where are you originally from?" Jack asked.

"Zielona Gora. You ever been?"

"No, but I hear it's really nice in summer."

"It's decent enough I suppose. And you? Warsaw?"

"I really am conspicuous."

"Something like that. What line of work you in?"

"Construction. I'm here for a meeting with new clients." Jack took a gulp of beer. "Have you moved around a lot?"

"A bit."

"Must have seen a few interesting places along the way."

"None worth talking about that much. Mind you, my daughter likes being on the move. I guess that's the traveller in her."

Jack didn't know if that was meant as a joke or not.

"She works with you?"

The barman's expression flickered with amusement, both hands disappearing beneath his apron. "When she isn't out cavorting with the natives," he paused, the door opening, "talk of the devil."

Jack glanced round as two people staggered into the bar. It was the drunk couple.

"Shut that thing, will you. You're letting out all the heat," the barman shouted.

The man appeared confused, almost toppling over trying to do as instructed.

"He's had too much," the barman muttered to Jack.

The barman's daughter pulled her companion to one side. She slammed the door shut with surprising ease, before shoving her friend into a chair. Her cheekbones were razors in a face which possessed a bony porcelain architecture. Her complexion paled further against a mane of black hair running down the length of her back.

"What can I say. He was thirsty," she said.

She was taller than Jack by several inches, almost a foot taller than her friend, whose head lolled against the wall.

"Why is it this generation never know when to stop?" the barman asked.

The woman strode across the room, pushing her hair from her shoulders, dislodging specks of snow, which melted on contact with the patched linoleum floor.

"Lack of discipline," she laughed.

Jack grabbed his coat, threw it on the bar.

"Let me guess. The old man's been boring you to tears with yet more tales of his travels?" she asked.

"Quite the opposite, in fact."

"Amazing," she said, asking her father to pour her a whiskey and coke. "Where you from?"

"It's the coat, right?"

She smiled.

"Afraid so."

From one of the pool tables voices grew animated as men tussled over a single cue.

"They had much?" she asked her father.

"Just the usual," he replied. "I'll go over and speak to them."

The barman left them alone.

"What a dump," she said.

Jack shrugged his shoulders apologetically as if he were responsible. The taxi ride from the station had shown him just how deeply the architecture affected the people, its inhabitants circling its streets as if summoned by unknown forces wanting them to contemplate the misery of their surroundings.

The barman's daughter swung herself onto the unoccupied stool.

"Jack," he said.

"Eva."

"If this place is as bad you say it is, what do you do for fun?"

"Drink, smoke, and listen to the locals moan. That's about as much fun as there is to be had round here."

He raised his glass for a toast.

"To boredom."

Eva did the same.

"Boredom."

They drank, watching each other over their glasses.

"Are you in block 49?"

He nodded.

"He's from your block." Eva looked over her shoulder at the figure sleeping by the entrance.

"I was beginning to think I was the only person in there," Jack said.

"Lucky you."

A sudden draft of cold air swept across the room. Jack turned to see two men standing in the open doorway.

"Here we go again," Eva said, getting up from her stool.

The two men had the same identical blank expressions and yellowish substance congealed about their stubble encrusted mouths. Even their skin had the same greyish quality matching the ingrained grubbiness of their clothes.

"Leave it to me," the barman said, emerging from the stockroom.

Eva returned to her stool.

"What do they want?" Jack asked.

"Something to drink, something to eat, the usual."

The barman approached the two men.

"Come back closing time."

One of them stepped forward, scabby lips twisting into what might have been a snarl or a reply. Eva got up from her stool again.

"You heard my father."

The other man took his friend's elbow and guided him back out of the door, closing it behind them.

"Sorry, about that," the barman said, "but sometimes you have to be firm."

"We get them in here all the time," Eva said, "only we don't want them scaring off the customers, so we ask them to come back when we're about to close up for the night."

"They seemed harmless enough."

"Oh, you'd be surprised sometimes."

Eva's father interrupted her.

"Ignore her. She's got her mother's looks, but I'm afraid to say, she's also got her mother's prejudices."

"You wish."

Jack looked at his empty pint glass again.

"I should head off."

"Can't tempt you with another?" the barman asked.

"Maybe tomorrow."

The barman glanced at the sleeping figure by the door.

"I don't suppose you'd give my daughter a hand with sleeping beauty over there?"

"Dad, stop it. I can manage him on my own."

Jack slipped on his coat.

"It's not a problem," he replied.

"Are you sure?" she asked.

"Like you say, he's in my block."

Together they got Eva's boyfriend to his feet and walked him out of the bar. Snow gusted past.

"Are you okay your side?" Eva asked.

"I'm fine. He's dead on his feet, a bit awkward."

"He's like this awake."

Jack laughed, the wind whipping the sound away. He stole a quick glance at her flawless skin, the shining whiteness of her teeth.

In the lift, she went through her boyfriend's pockets for the keys to his flat.

"Sorry about this," she said.

"No problem, happy to help."

So long as I get to spend a bit more time with you, Jack thought, but was far too afraid to say this out loud, and not only because of what she might say.

Eva found the keys, and as they entered the flat, she switched on a light. They lowered the boyfriend onto a threadbare monstrosity, presumably a sofa. Jack surveyed the room, the mess. It made his stomach turn. Piles of unwashed clothing lay on the floor next to plates of unfinished food. A large ceramic bowl filled with black water sat by the door. Jack was lucky he hadn't kicked it over entering the room.

"Will you be alright with him now?"

"You're going?"

He suppressed a shudder, the room making him feel sick. Jack had his problems, but this place was disgusting. He detested bad hygiene.

"I've got an early start."

"He's not my boyfriend, if that's what you're thinking."

"I wasn't thinking anything except I need to go to bed."

He walked into the hallway. Eva followed him.

"Sorry that sounded rude," he said. A greater temptation was rising above his need for alcohol, and he heard the words before he properly considered where they might lead him. "How about a coffee and a bite to eat tomorrow? Somewhere in town, somewhere a bit more convivial?"

Eva gave him a smile, before describing a café in the main town square.

"See you tomorrow then," Jack said, closing the door.

*

The next morning, Eva was leaving the bar the back way through the stockroom when she found Adrian crouched down at the side of the fire exit, clutching the handrail.

"I see you're up and about again. Although judging from the state of you last night, God knows how."

Dried vomit coloured the ground at his feet, while uncombed hair plastered his sweating forehead.

"Lover boy's back," a voice said. Her father stepped past her through the doorway. "This one doesn't know when to stop."

"That's his problem."

"I don't want him hanging around outside."

Eva glanced at her phone.

"I've got to be in town in twenty minutes."

Her father gave her that look, the one which said she'd no choice.

*

Jack found the cafe easily enough, a wicker basket with dead flowers hanging above the doorway. Inside the tables were empty. Jack rang the bell on the counter as a flimsy piece of debris flew past the window.

"We're closing up for the day."

A thin woman shuffled out of a doorway. At the corner of her mouth a tiny yellow spot caught his attention.

"I was supposed to be meeting a friend here."

"Nobody's been in."

"Are you sure?"

"As I'll ever be."

The woman traipsed after him, escorting him out of the door, her rudeness forgotten when he checked his phone for messages. *Really sorry, got caught up with something unexpected. Can we meet tonight at your place? Eva.*

The town square was a scene of wintry paralysis, a snow choked fountain protruding from the ground, outdoor ice-covered tables resembling metallic skeletons. He walked through the streets, every so often a distant figure materialising ahead of him, trudging out of reach. Jack finally gave up his pursuit of invisible people and phoned a taxi. While he waited outside a derelict supermarket with boarded-up windows, he contemplated sending a reply to Eva.

The taxi pulled up. Jack got into the front seat.

"Anywhere special?" the driver asked, a gloved hand touching a yellow spot at the corner of his mouth.

*

The shop assistant said nothing when he asked for a bottle of Glenfiddich, merely scratched at the yellow spot on her lower lip. He paid in cash, because using his card would only alert Sylvia if she checked their joint bank account. Walking to the block, the sky came awake with snowfall.

In the warmth of the flat, he considered calling Eva. He was unsure of what he'd say, unused to retracing his steps with people when sober. Have a quick drink first, get your spirits up, quite literally. Whiskey will help, it always does.

*

There was laughter. Faces too. They converged on him with quickening intensity, hands mauling, or were they embracing him? It was hard to say since his mouth no longer worked. The barman's face floated past, those horrible long yellow nails of his slicing at the bloated belly of an elderly man slouched in a chair in the middle of the bar, people gathered around him, watching as his innards slopped out.

Before Jack could object with his dead tongue, he was creeping up on Eva to surprise her with his presence.

"You're such a relic," she said without turning around.

He halted in the middle of the room, listening to her words, but not really understanding what she meant.

"In a way, you're a bit like this place, these people. If it wasn't for the fact that I like you so much, despite your faults, I'd say you belonged here."

She turned around, gesturing to the man asleep on the sofa, whose face was as delicate as a papier-mâché mask

*

Jack woke up in a place he at first didn't recognise, not until he realised he was sitting in a chair in the bar. An empty bottle of whisky stood on a table in front of him. It was early morning, still dark outside. Snow fell in lazy windblown patterns past the windows. His hangover beat the inside of his head, making his eyes swim. Behind the bar, a fringe of light came from under the stockroom door.

He remembered nothing about how he'd ended up here, or even when? The whiskey was to blame, until he glanced at the bottle and realised it was Starka whiskey, not Glenfiddich. Okay, definitely the whiskey.

Jack got to his feet, walked over to the stockroom and pushed open the door. He was expecting to see Eva unloading crates of bottles. Instead he saw her father, who was standing over a woman kneeling on the floor.

"Almost done. This one's the last," the barman said, who realised his mistake and smiled at Jack calmly.

The barman was naked from the waist up, skinny arms outstretched in monstrous supplication. His ribs, clear beneath the waxy substance of his flesh, moved like cogs in a machine grinding together. He gripped one end of a distended translucent appendage protruding from his hairless chest.

"Fancy a taste?" the barman asked.

Jack lurched out of the stockroom and across the bar, colliding with the table with the whiskey bottle. He flung the door open as the bottle smashed onto the floor. The freezing cold hit him in the face with such force, sobriety was a blast of arctic temperature, like rubbing sandpaper across his eyeballs.

Outside the bar, people were shuffling through the snow, moving with the dispirited familiarity of drunks. A woman, the whites of her eyes showing, blinded to his presence, cried out. Possibly she could hear Jack trampling through the snow. He pushed past her, confronted by a boy crawling on his hands and knees. High up in one of the blocks, a window shattered and a metal chair sailed through the air, landing in a wreckage of twisted legs.

"Help me!" someone shouted.

Jack leapt over the boy, chubby hands reaching for him.

When he reached his block, he saw even more people indiscriminately circling one another, partially dressed, limbs blue from exposure.

Entering the block, he realised he didn't have his phone. He got out of the lift on his floor and managed to get his key out, when an old man appeared in the doorway opposite.

"We have something for you," the old man said.

Behind him a young woman clutched a tiny bundle wrapped in a blanket. The corridor light faltered, shadows leaping across the ceiling. The old man leaned out into the corridor, hands scrambling at the doorposts. The woman side-stepped him into the corridor, letting the blanket fall open. A pink, viscous heap of matter hit the floor with an audible thwack.

Jack slammed the door shut behind him, locking it.

"This is what happens when people don't know when to stop."

Eva was waiting for him, motioning to the remains of her boyfriend, who was now nothing more than liquefied flesh dribbling off the sofa and onto the floor. Jack grabbed at the wall, his chest constricting, knowing it was pointless to run.

"I thought you might appreciate what was going on around here. After last night, after seeing the state you got yourself in, I decided you were ready for this." She was on her feet and moving across the room before he could react, long hands stroking a malformed lump beneath her clothes.

Jack wiped his mouth.

"Which is what?"

She stopped moving, grabbed his hand and placed it on the bump beneath her clothes.

"Why, satiation of course."

THE SEAT

The climb up the hillside had left Vincent exhausted. He lay in the morning sun in the grass, his backpack beside him. Below the Polish countryside spread out among a cornucopia of yellow and green vegetation. He squinted at the church. Its shadow stopped within inches of where he lay, a line of demarcation. He climbed to his feet, itching to get inside, only slowed down by old expectations. Caution. The hillside fell towards the Odra which was a distant glimmer among a tide of greenery. He remembered visiting the river months earlier and standing on its narrow banks, watching the slate grey water coiling through reeds with hypnotic calm.

He cupped his hands over his mouth and yelled. His voice rang out among the surrounding hills. He was probably the only person for miles around.

The church was far from the dilapidated ruin he'd been expecting. The bell-tower, atop of which sat a gleaming onion dome with spire, repudiated its history. Yet the location troubled him, situated as it was on a hillside miles from anywhere.

In the graveyard, he found headstones which jutted from the earth as if ruinous teeth, inscriptions worn smooth, impossible to decipher. Whoever lay in these graves did so without voice or title. Nearby a juniper tree wilted in the shadow of the church. He had a disconcerting feeling the church was emptying out the accumulated poisons of centuries, while neglect flowered everywhere else.

The church door was unlocked, exactly as she said it would be. How could she have known that would still be the case? Instinctively he reached for the font inside the entrance, dabbing at water which was no longer there. Daylight fell through arched windows into a gloom beneath thick wooden rafters, the air smelling of dust and age. He'd imagined it would resemble the one from his childhood, completely unprepared for its sparse walls and uncloaked altar, deprived as it was of its customary exaggerations, stripped bare. There was none of the awful malformed iconography which had once transfixed him. No more dying Christ figures in gilded opulence, no more morose symbols comprising the inscrutable puzzle of his religious upbringing.

Standing here brought back memories of forlorn communion processions, disheartened parishioners shuffling along with the weariness of condemned prisoners, parents prodding their children away from them as if specimens of some unbearable guilt. Such a stifling pageant of faith.

He counted the pews. There were twenty either side of the nave, facing one another as they rose into the dusty sunlight. It wasn't anything like Saint Luke's chapel, not really, except for the arrangement of the pews. He looked towards the church entrance, above which was a wooden viewing gallery. The remoteness of the church made him wonder if there had ever been enough people to necessitate its inclusion. Only it wasn't this which interested him so much as the hole carved out of the wall above it.

One year ago, Vincent had been forced into visiting his own city university. His girlfriend had been the reason, appalled by the revelation he'd *never set foot inside such a world renowned educational institution*.

"I live here. Why would I want to?"

"It's a bit embarrassing," Natalie goaded.

"For you and your snobby friends perhaps."

She pulled a shocked face, an exaggeration of real feelings.

"I want to go and see," she said, undeterred as always.

Seldom steered off course, Natalie had swiftly arranged a tour for the next week. They argued about it several times before they went, only it wasn't the real reason for their differences.

Their guide was an elderly, grey-haired woman called Irene. A fellow, she'd conducted their small group through the university grounds, politely answering questions and relaying anecdotal stories, while pointing out interesting architecture, before concluding the visit in Saint Luke's chapel.

On entering the chapel, Vincent noted the pews, facing one another across the nave, and not towards the altar as in traditional churches. Irene saw his confusion, explaining this was because students should acknowledge the provosts as they arrived for mass. The tour guide then indicated a space built into the wall beside the entrance.

"What is?"

The guide smiled.

"Why, it's a seat of course. For the provost no less."

Vincent stared at the large hole roughly hewn out of the wall above the viewing gallery. Was this really the same thing? And if so, who had it been intended for?

A week after the university tour, Vincent had bumped into Irene in Oxford city centre.

"Small world," she said, with a hint of a smile.

She was carrying two large shopping bags. Although she was far from frail looking, there was something in her face which said she was struggling not to show how tired she really was.

"Here, let me take those," he said.

She didn't object, and together they walked out of the city and into the suburbs. By the time they reached her street, for some reason he'd unravelled the majority of the problems currently entangling his life. It was unlike him to be this forthcoming, so out of character even Natalie would have felt compelled to ask. They'd stood at the end of her nondescript driveway, chewing over his pronouncements on relationships, his confusion at what he was going to do.

"I can help," Irene had said.

It had seemed a mere politeness to say anything to him at this point, only the way she spoke made him think differently.

It didn't take long, not more than five minutes really. It should have been absurd, for it made no sense. Rationally speaking that was. Except lying in bed that night, Irene's words floated around inside his head.

A week later, and without telling Natalie, Vincent quit his job and enrolled on a TEFL teaching course at the local college. The strange thing was he didn't feel in the slightest bit guilty. And by this stage it was too late for her to be able to change his mind.

After he broke up with Natalie, he moved back to his parents for a month. It wasn't long before he landed a job in a private language school in a town situated in the west of Poland, exactly as Irene had instructed.

"Approximately fifteen miles from the town of Zielona Gora, you'll find what you want there. The Holy Magdalena, located in the middle of the Polish countryside."

"Find what?"

"The thing which is missing."

"But what is it?"

"A church, on a hill. I came across it on a rambling holiday twenty years ago."

Eight months passed, eight months in which he rarely thought about the church. He adapted quickly to his new surrounding, settling into Polish life with unanticipated ease. No one was more surprised by this than Vincent. In many ways it renewed him, made him happy to be there. His colleagues, a mixture of native speakers and Polish teachers were a disparate collection, all of whom had their own peculiar nuances. He fit right in.

It was going so much better than he had dared to imagine that soon Irene's words were just a memory and not an instruction. Until two mornings ago, when he sat up on one elbow and realised his girlfriend was watching him with grim fascination from the other side of the bed.

"Do you remember what you told me before you fell asleep?" Joanna asked.

He'd been praying she might have ignored him this morning just so he didn't have to confront the repetition.

"You said you were bored of everything. Does that mean me?"

"Of course not."

"Then what did you mean by it?"

"Look, I've got lessons in a couple of hours. Can we talk about this later? I really don't have the time to have an argument about absolutely nothing."

He watched her threw on her clothes and storm out of her bedroom and into the kitchen flat without a backward glance. She ignored his calls for two days, until the day he was climbing onto a PKS bus.

"I'm sorry about the other day," he said.

She listened to his explanation, although what he said was illogical even to his own ears.

"I need to do it alone."

"Really?"

"I know how all this sounds."

"It doesn't make any sense."

"I know that."

A noise brought him back to the present, away from whatever regrets he was experiencing. At first he thought it was mice, or perhaps a bird trapped inside the church walls. He looked up at the hole in the wall. It was a protracted rustling, reminding him of somebody unfurling a heavy raincoat and hanging it out to dry. For some unexplainable reason he imagined something clambering out of the hole.

Then he heard some altogether different, a wet slithering sound working its way across the floor of the viewing gallery. Not slithering, squirming.

If you stay, you won't have to guess for much longer. You'll soon see what's up there.

Vincent grabbed his backpack and walked hurriedly to the entrance. The door was ajar. Had he left it open? It was like looking at a painting, the countryside framed by the doorposts, the hills sat in bright sunshine, comforting enough to dispel what his imagination wanted him to think.

He closed the door after him, pausing a second, waiting to see what might happen if anything, more than relieved when nobody began tugging at it from the other side. However, as he entered the graveyard, he heard it open.

He looked back, knew he shouldn't have, but a sickening curiosity had hold of him. A shadow darkened the doorway and fell onto the path, blackening so suddenly it was like watching a cloud descend from the sky. Was that someone crouched low in the doorway? It was hard saying what he could see from this distance. He should have felt safe under the bright cloudless sky, instead he felt as if someone had plunged him into a pool of darkness he could only perceive.

He walked briskly through the graveyard, not running, not yet, eyes staring straight ahead. Only when he reached the path did he glance over his shoulder. There was no longer anyone standing in the church doorway if there ever had been.

He scanned the graveyard, convinced they were lurking nearby, ready to pop up like a malevolent jack-in-the-box. Grass stirred in the breeze, insects droning contentedly. Was he hoping to catch sight of whoever it was?

Trees whipped by as he descended the hill. A bead of sweat caught in the hollow of his throat, trickling into his chest hair. Shapes lunged out of the undergrowth; the carcasses of trees, a rock wall scattered in sections.

As if willed into existence the roadside appeared, a small wooden footbridge between him and its embankment. He ran across the bridge, planks jigging at his weight. Halfway up the embankment, he heard the planks jump again, the exact same sound it had made moments before.

This time Vincent fought every molecule of his personality against looking back.

A PKS bus materialized, windows glinting in the sun. He tore along the grassy verge, waving his arms, convinced the bus would drive away, leave him stranded there. The vehicle idled, teasing him with its proximity, the driver leaning over the steering wheel, watching him.

Vincent clambered up its steps out of breath, uncaring the other passengers were gawping at him. He showed his pass and slumped down into a seat. They pulled out into the road and passed the deserted footbridge.

The church leaned out from the hillside as if enquiring of his whereabouts.

*

When he arrived back in Zielona Gora, he realised he'd completely forgotten it was Winobranie. The yearly wine festival attracted people from all over the country, the town plunged into a week long state of drunken debauchery. Or that was how Joanna had jokingly described it. He'd barely noticed people setting up their market stalls this morning, so focused as he was on finding the church.

People staggered past in fancy dress costumes, pursuing one another with awkward good humour. Numerous market stalls clogged the avenues, selling traditional Polish food, cheap jewellery, and cheaper wine. On some stalls ribald women paraded hideous fashions, while every few yards the canopies of beer tents rippled with drinkers. Vincent detested crowds, the idea of being folded into himself was horrifying.

He rang Joanna, agreeing to meet in a pub close to her flat. Usually it would have been standing room only, but the wine festival meant it would be empty of regulars.

"I'll give Kasia a call. Maybe she'll bring Pawel with her. He's nice, you'll like him. He's desperate to try out his English on a native speaker."

Part of him wasn't in the mood for company, but at the same time he felt better knowing there would be more people around him tonight.

*

The first of many blocks reared above him, a hulk of shadow falling on the smaller buildings below. Doors clattered open while others rattled shut, conversations from open windows thrown out into the night, a language whose understated distinctions hinted at something he wasn't yet skilled enough to understand.

It was close to nightfall when he reached his own block, the street quieter than usual. He stood with his key in hand, waiting, only for what? *The church on the hill. You will find what you want there.* Or had she said, you'll find what you *need* there? He couldn't remember anymore.

There was a house across the street from his block, one which had been unoccupied for as long as he'd been living here. Its windows flickered with the reflection of street lights. And something else maybe?

*

Vincent found Joanna and friends sitting in a corner drinking beer from pitchers. On the wall above their table was a mirror in which his twin approached with visible trepidation. The door through which he'd just entered closed behind him on a street that was swelling with darkness. *It's waiting for me*, he thought, as crazy as that sounded. He launched into a conversation almost the second he sat down and introduced himself to Pawel. Joanna gave him a cautious glance, but said nothing.

They left the pub shortly before eleven o'clock, walking back to Joanna's flat.

"Are you sure? Yours is nearer," she pointed out.

"We agreed. One day your place, one day mine. Today's your turn."

Vincent was relieved they could avoid his flat for tonight. He didn't know why, and didn't really want to think about it too much. He was tired of over analysing everything.

On the way he explained to Joanna what he thought he might have witnessed at the church.

"I think Irene was pulling my leg," he said.

"Eccentrics the whole lot of you," she replied, smiling.

He appreciated she was trying to alleviate some of his fears, which he wasn't entirely certain could be adequately described.

"If it's just that, then it wasn't for nothing," he pointed out, squeezing her hand.

Joanna listened quietly as he spoke, never once showing the slightest doubt he was telling the truth. She never attempted to speak over him, or make him feel as if he what he was saying was being scrutinized for inaccuracies. She was the complete opposite of Natalie in every way.

She was by far the smartest person he knew. With a PhD in chemical engineering, and not to mention her English was pratically flawless, he often wondered why she was with him. Not in some plaintive, *oh why me* melancholic spiel intended to draw out compliments, but because he genuinely struggled to see what he had to offer.

Once they were in bed, Vincent felt less afraid, or less afraid of the thing he couldn't put into words.

"Do you feel like you can rest now?"

"I wish I'd never been there," he said.

She stared at him, possibly taken aback by his response.

"The funny thing about that place is who was the so called seat for?"

"What do you mean?"

"I only thought about it later, but I didn't see any stairs to the viewing gallery."

"Then maybe it wasn't a viewing gallery at all."

Joanna put her head on the pillow next to his.

"Let's sleep."

They closed their eyes, his hand on her hips, feeling the warmth of her body until he was asleep.

*

Vincent watched light from the street claw entry through the curtains. A radiator let out a sigh, the darkness shifting as his eyes adjusted.

"Can't you sleep?"

Joanna's voice startled him.

"Sorry. Must be the beer, it always has the opposite effect on me."

"I've got cigarettes."

Although he had quit smoking just before leaving the UK, he sometimes succumbed when under stress. Earlier that evening at the pub, he'd had a cigarette outside the main entrance with Pawel, not really paying attention to what he was saying, one eye on the rapidly vanishing town lights.

"Good idea."

"Don't let it become a habit though."

"Says the social smoker."

"Go look in my coat," she said, without changing her position.

Joanna's coat hung on the back of the kitchen door. He searched through the pockets, fingers pulling at receipts, until he found the cigarette pack.

Vincent stood by the kitchen window, the latch open to let the smoke out. There was nothing to see but stationary cars, a comforting normality. Except inside the abandoned house on the other side of the street a blackness stirred. He closed the blinds on it.

When he climbed back into bed, Joanna was already fast asleep. As he lay down next to her, a street light flared outside the window, darkness rushing into the room. He hadn't noticed he still had the cigarette lighter in his hand, almost as if he'd returned to the room prepared.

For what?

He rubbed at the flint, a spark flashing temporary illumination. It went out much too quickly for him to see anything. He tried again. A flame appeared, shadows writhing at the foot of the bed. The flame went out once more, gas sloshing around inside the plastic container.

"Joanna, you awake?"

There was no answer. He put a hand on her shoulder and gently shook her. Still no reaction. Then again, she was a deep sleeper, especially compared to him.

He tried the lighter once more. Longer illumination this time, a hazy orange circle wavering on the ceiling.

Blackness rose above the bed, becoming something more substantial. Vincent closed his eyes. There was no time for anything else.

THE PLACES

In his dreams, Ken remembers the coal bunker clotted with cobwebs, coal-dust caught between the strands like falling black stars in cosmic paralysis. In his dreams, he hears a car in the suburban street above, street lamps threatening illumination through the opening by which he's gained entry, him the teenage phantom returning to other people's graves. He stumbles around, picking up objects, shining his pocket torch at the floor like a detective from the tawdry paperbacks his father loves to read—half a brick, a lump of coal, a sports paper dated 1973, its colours having run together with the pages—searching for something he can return to school with the next day.

Paul stopped typing, looking up from his laptop and out the window of his hotel room. At a bus-stop across the street, a double-decker emptied school children onto the pavement, their energetic voices resembling arias in minor operatic works. He envied them, naive as to why. He returned to the book, the looming deadline forcing him to confront his annoyance at having to work in a way he wasn't used to.

In the coal bunker, an old boiler stands rusting under several zinc coats. Behind it a section of wall has come away like a temptation to venture further than he has already. Damp air blows through the hole, the passage beyond the source of numerous playground stories. He imagines scattered bones, a greying skull patched with moss, eye sockets empty of thought.

He's doing all of this for the approval of boys he won't recognise ten years on, boys without the remotest understanding of what it has taken for him to come here alone, how it feels to sneak down into the darkness beneath the church at night, unaided by the false camaraderie of boyhood. Ken hates school, but no more so than he hates the too few friendships which have become mere conveniences to survive it.

There in the miserable cloying darkness it occurs to him he's consciously trading one part of his life for the possibility of another. Despite the destruction maturity will bring, such as the failed panoply of innumerable relationships to come (he thinks of the foggy atmosphere of his parents' marriage, or the male pageantry his lovely Aunt Lorraine submits herself to on a weekly basis), he'll gladly accept such uncertainties. It is better than the primitive assertions children are forced to endure of the so called rites of passage.

He bends down to the floor, convinced he can see something shining in the dark, when a section of the boiler wall collapses onto him, burying him in darkness.

Paul stared at the screen knowing he'd have to erase those last few paragraphs because his editor would never believe any teenager possessed such a vocabulary, not even a Graham Greene prototype. His debut novel, *Urban Murder,* had landed him decent reviews and made him money. Nonetheless, this next book, part of a contracted series, was going to ruin him creatively if he didn't soon do something else.

*

When he saw the sign for Chapel Hill, he rang Angela saying he'd collect Christopher from school.

"How far away are you?"

"Almost there."

"I thought you were coming straight home first?"

Angela had innate suspicion woven into her DNA, and any answer Paul gave plunged her into self-doubt.

"I *am* home," he chimed, making a joke of it.

"You know what I mean. I still don't know why you had to get a hotel. You could have driven back last night." Her rising voice counterpointed his faked cheeriness.

Last night Paul had been one of several guests discussing the state of publishing on Arts Particular on Radio Merseyside. What he'd neglected to tell his wife was the interview had been recorded in the morning.

"I went for drinks with the other guests. The BBC were paying, so I could hardly pass it up now, could I?"

He wasn't going to tell her he'd wanted an evening alone, even if it had been spent writing.

He parked two streets away from the school, the roads blocked with parents' cars. In the five minutes it took to walk there, talking to Angela was like trying to persuade a potential suicide down from a ledge.

"Got to go," he said, wanting to end the conversation before he said something he'd later come to regret.

"Is something wrong?"

Her endless questions exhausted him. He wanted to say: *I have dreamed of taking*

Christopher away from you, before it's too late, before you turn him into a copy of you.

"Nothing's wrong. I'm at the school now," he said, ending the call.

She wouldn't ring back, not straight away, that would seem too desperate. She'd pretend his phone battery had died. After a few minutes of full-blown paranoia, she'd dial his number so fast her hands would be shaking. He felt like a bastard for thinking these things and called her back. She picked up before the first ring completed.

"Bloody phones," he said.

She laughed nervously. Was he on the verge of gas-lighting his own wife? She'd been behaving like this for months on end, becoming increasingly panicky. He was only trying to preserve the balance, not tip her over the edge.

She grasped at his explanation as if believing him. "I sometimes wonder if we're better off without."

He thought she meant him, before realising she was talking about phones in general.

"Christopher will be out in a second."

He couldn't control the frustration in his voice any more than Angela could describe the emotions strangling her logic.

"Are you there?"

"You need to let me go now, Angela?"

There was an intake of breath.

"He missed you."

He waited for her to add, *I missed you too*. Perhaps she knew she was pushing her luck, because she said nothing more.

"We'll be home soon," he said.

One of Christopher's classmates ran past screaming laughter.

"What was that? I couldn't hear."

"See you in a bit."

"I'll get something nice on," she said.

He followed the metal railings around the school playing fields with its spread of interconnected buildings and prefabricated huts. Except for the metal fence, it hadn't changed in twenty years or more.

His son appeared on the other side of the railings, stippled by the sun through the bars. The electronic gate opened, Christopher grabbing his father's hand. They walked along a path shaded by elms, a side street of semi-detached council houses built sometime shortly after the war.

"That's where your mum grew up," he said, pointing at one house. In the garden of number thirteen, a teenage girl knelt in the driveway fixing the engine of her motorbike.

The house looked nothing at all like it did in the photographs Angela had once shown him. Long ago there'd been a tree in the front garden, its branches overspreading the pavement like a downturned palm.

His son blinked thoughtfully.

"Nan's house."

"Good boy."

There was a distant rumble, a train heading to Kirby or Manchester, the sound reminding him of last night's dream. He'd been standing in waist high grass in the middle of a field, lightning flickering in the sky all around him.

At home Angela prodded him with a few questions, her original suspicions persisting. Their son watched from the floor of the living room while colouring a giraffe in a book. Paul thought his son understood, even if his shy, furtive glances reminded him of Angela.

"Whoops." Angela interrupted his thoughts, deliberately he guessed.

Her blonde hair covered one side of her face as she picked up a downed salt-seller, brushing the spilled salt into a napkin.

"If I was the superstitious kind," she joked.

She stood at the kitchen counter rolling flour onto a pastry board, surrounded by plastic containers, a manic overspill describing how she usually behaved.

"Are you going to do some writing later?

"I'll go for a run first," he said.

She unfolded the napkin and shook it out.

"A run will do you good, help you to think," she said.

He searched her face for proof of the accusation she was holding back.

*

He had several established routes for his runs, one of which took him along an overgrown bridle path, a leafy avenue of trees between a hedgerow and a sports field. A teenage girl stepped out in front of him, forcing him to go around her.

"Sorry," he said over his shoulder.

Her angular face had a long fringe, a style he hadn't seen in years.

"Everybody's there, but you," she yelled after him.

He turned to look back at her, the girl standing in exactly the same spot as if paralyzed by the sight of him.

"Excuse me?"

She disappeared behind a tree, hiding. He sighed, feeling sorry for her. One more broken personality left wandering the streets.

Where were her parents? Her friends? Probably she had none.

Pretending to tie his laces, he waited for her to reappear. She didn't, and he guessed she was unlikely to do so while he was standing there.

Jogging off the bridle path into an adjoining street, he passed a residential home. A row of elderly women sat in armchairs looking out the windows. Were they staring at their own reflections or something else?

He followed their gaze but saw only the bridle path, its overgrown hedgerows gently blowing in the wind.

*

In the last week of February, Ken has been elevated to the forefront of other people's conversations, cajoled into recounting his night spent unconscious in the coal bunker beneath the church. His accident has exposed him to a surge of morbid curiosity, inadvertently raising him up to an altogether discernible height. And while he's never experienced real popularity, he's at least able to distance himself from the faceless crowd he's been a part of for so long.

A month later, and somebody else is pushed out into the fickle spotlight of popularity. Although Ken's conversion remains intact, interest in him wanes just as he knew it would. These have always been the rules of school for as long as anybody can remember. Tracing the source of these unspoken tenets can at best prove to be elusive, akin to Old World explorers groping their way through unchartered jungles without the slightest clue into which direction they're heading.

Paul saved his work and went downstairs to find Angela in the garden half dozing in a deck chair. Christopher was sitting at her feet, drawing on a piece of paper. Neither of them noticed he was there, when his phone started ringing.

One of Angela's legs kicked out, startled by the sudden intrusion of noise.

The street lights in the avenue backing onto their garden came on with an audible hum.

"Hello?" he asked the unidentified caller.

"You belong in the places," a voice said.

He pictures their grimacing faces, all of them tricked into emoting something far larger than they're used to. Three teenagers in a field of waist high grass, the sky an unpleasant dark grey, lightning spearing its bleak clouds. In front of them, a figure crouches on a mound of soil, into which it thrusts its hands, searching.

It looks at them.

"All of you belong in the places."

Paul was no longer outside in the garden. He was sitting at his desk in his *writing room* as Angela called it. The computer was on, the screen filled with words he'd no memory of writing. Tacked to the wall above his desk was a Polaroid photograph showing three teenagers standing in a field.

He began to type again.

*

His mother tucks the blanket between the mattress and the base, smoothing it out. She tiptoes away, unaware Ken has been watching her the whole time.

"Goodnight, mum. Love you."

She doesn't hear him, and closes the door.

From downstairs, his dad's voice is a low insistent vibration coming up through the floorboards, a voice asking too many questions. Nevertheless, knowing he's there, the sound insulates Ken, makes him feel safe.

A pane in the window rattles against the frame. It's raining again, the wind blowing, miserable weather. He doesn't want to have to think about what might have happened if the caretaker hadn't found him. The feelings are worse than the experience, manifest wounds left to rankle like a medieval injury, reeling him from sleep.

Something drips onto his forehead. He looks up, sees a face above his own, eyes darting.

"Need you back where you started out from," it says, its mouth is a cruel abnormality.

Ken screams. Footsteps come up the stairs as the thing scrambles up the wall and scuttles into a corner over his bed, folding itself inwards, a cocoon made from its own limbs. Only a patch of shimmering blackness remains of its presence.

His parents rush into the room, light spilling in from the landing, Ken jabbing a finger into the air.

"There, there, there."

But whatever he think he's seen has vanished.

*

A crust of moonlight appeared in the window, the photograph now an outline without details. Paul was too afraid to turn on the desk lamp in case of what else it might reveal. The computer screen glowed, drawing him to it.

*

Ken's father reads the front page of the local newspaper aloud.

"Terry Parkinson was last seen walking on Druid Hill Lane..."

"Do you think they're connected?" Ken's mum interrupts.

There have been several disappearances in the last few years in the village. Toby Leyland, Andrea Leyland and now Terry Parkinson. Ken thinks he knows why these people in particular. Toby had survived a serious car crash and been feted like a baronial lord by his classmates. Andrea, a sixth former with realistic pretensions of going to Oxford or Cambridge, by all accounts a shut-in, had taken an overdose of her mother's sleeping pills, and become momentarily popular for all the wrong reasons. Terry had been attacked by a gang from a neighbouring village, and spent three weeks on life support, later acquiring friends he'd no idea he had. For a short time, these were familiar names in the national press, whose disappearances had culminated in extensive searches of the surrounding countryside, although no trace was ever found of them.

"Everybody knows how these things usually turn out," Ken's dad says. He's right,

these things always turn out the way everyone imagines, even when they try not to think about it too much.

Ken doesn't dare tell his parents about the note he found stuffed into his geography folder. **There are places for people like you**. *That's what it says. He has spent days telling himself it means nothing, that the popular kids have reneged on their acceptance of him by pulling a vague prank he cannot grasp.*

But as he refuses to speculate, his sleeping mind speculates for him. And so something begins to stalk him, growing less hazy and much more recognizable as his nightmares shunt up into the alarming brightness of reality.

He can't say for certain who's following him, for there's nothing to point at, no face to attach a name to, no physical presence whose personality will be easy to decipher from the expressions they wear. There's only the lengthening of days, of children in the streets on their bicycles, of teenage romances snuffed out quicker than the time it takes to cultivate them, the usual elements of his world. And yet there's something there. Watching him. He senses it hiding around every corner, behind every closed door, a sound in the distance, a voice, someone calling his name. Over and over and over again.

Ken changes his route home, no longer cutting through the allotments or taking the path behind the council rented garages. He stays in plain sight, uses the main roads, the most populated streets, making sure he's always within shouting distance of an adult. This is his plan, and as unlikely as it seems that he can outwit it, he must at least try.

*

Paul found Angela at the bottom of the stairs clutching Christopher, whose head sagged against her shoulder.

"It wanted him," she said.

He knelt down, stroking Christopher's hair out of his eyes.

"I'm so sorry, son."

Christopher buried his head into his mother's chest, refusing to surface despite whatever assurance Paul could give him.

"How long have you known?" he asked Angela.

"Ever since you started the other book," she sighed, "if only you'd kept to the series."

On that night all those years ago, his failed attempt to break into the church vault had been to impress the boys in his class, not because he thought he could leapfrog the lesser path laid down for him. The commercial contract, the book signings, the radio interviews and fan letters, all of them were the inadvertent spoils created by this alternate path.

He reached for his son again, meaning to hug him, but his fingers scraped through the contours of his fading skull. Angela pleaded with him, the substance of her body an iridescent and vaporous extrication of floating particles, becoming less than she was.

"For your son," she said.

Paul stood up and walked out of the house.

People like him were never meant to be anything more than a footnote in the lives of their families.

*

Everything he remembered from that night was exactly as he recalled. Even the graveyard was untouched by the intervening years. He'd driven past the church thousands of times, but not until he'd started writing the new book had he given it any real thought.

The door to the coal bunker shouldn't have been open, not since the whole thing had been bricked up several days after his accident in the late 1980s. But there it was, his way back to an unfinished past.

He felt around inside the doorway for the box of Swan matches left there the first time, and lit the half melted candles protruding from a shelf. The hole in the wall gaped behind the boiler, darkness folding through it like a dark and deadly promise.

Paul lay down on the floor, smelling the coal dust in the air, seeing the ancient remnants of cobwebs above his head. The wall around the boiler trembled, bricks coming loose, ready to bury him one last time.

AND WHEN THE LIGHTS CAME ON

The last night of the job Artur walked between the large expensive houses not quite recognising them. At the end of the street a van with the district emblem printed on its doors was waiting for him. From the driver's window the faint tail of a cigarette flickered like the gas lamps he'd lit for the last time. The lamps were bright, but not so startling so as to cast the surrounding houses into complete exposure. As a child the dark had never frightened him, not with so many power shortages. He recalled lying in the blackness of his bedroom, tethered to the vestigial fragments of dreams.

"Hurry up there, Artur," said a voice from the van. The cigarette burned brightly, unlike the gas lamps.

In recent years, the street had become an unofficial tourist attraction. Several Polish TV productions had filmed there, until the locals had grown tired of seeing sightseers taking selfies outside their houses. This had led to a decision being made to connect the street to the electric grid. The gas lamps would remain, but no longer functional. What would the houses look like under the intrusive electric lights? Fixing the lighting pole to the van roof, he climbed into the van.

"Do you know how long I've been doing this?"

There was a considerable pause from the driver, long enough to insinuate either disinterest or caution.

Artur didn't know the driver's name, had never bothered asking it.

"A long time's my guess," came the reply.

The driver reversed the van, keeping his eyes on the road, the back of his head turned to Artur. In the glow of the dashboard, glossy lumps showed through shoulder length hair, strands matted with blood.

*

The day that Toll Street was connected to the electric grid, Artur received his medal for services to the state. It was a thick gaudy piece of metal, which the president of Warsaw hung round his neck while they were photographed. He was proud to be the last official gas lamp attendant in the whole of the city, and only wished Zuzanna had been alive to see it.

Hands shook their usual indifference, while expressions struggled politely against a backdrop of suits. Once the ceremony was over, he was more than relieved to make his way outside into the rain.

On a tram elderly ladies swathed in bulky coats haggled with younger people about their rights to a seat. Artur ignored them as everyone else was doing, preferring to watch the city slide by in submission to the weather. The capital was a much different city to the one he'd grown up in, shopping centres, office blocks, skyscrapers, transforming the skyline.

A drunk collapsed into the seat behind him, legs splayed at painful looking angles, not that anybody paid him any attention. The tram stuttered to a halt, smoke wafting from the undercarriage. Doors flapped open, Artur traipsing after the sulking mob of fellow passengers.

One street away from the underground station the rain returned, streaking office buildings. Arthur waited at a crossing for the lights to change.

On a billboard a half-naked model airbrushed to perfection sprawled across a marble staircase for reasons he couldn't fathom. Blood dripped from her eyes, dribbling down her face onto the pavement. Artur raised a leg towards the passing whine of traffic, a noise which increased as if smelling a sacrifice. A wing-mirror almost clipped him.

He arrived at the café ten minutes late. A middle-aged woman with a face like a reluctant mime artist uncertain of what she wanted to communicate, was waiting for him.

He sat down, pulling the lapels of his coat over his chest so as to hide the medal. He'd hadn't thought it important to invite his daughter to the ceremony. She was too like her mother, too eager to reassure him.

The waiter came over and took his order, his head gaping bloodily. It was several minutes before Artur realised his daughter was speaking.

"...looking for a babysitter or somebody..."

"What day do you want me?"

Ania placed her hand on the back of his heavily veined one, hopeless at appearing diffident. He wondered why Gregory had ever married her. Then he wished that thought away, disturbed by its ruthlessness.

When his daughter left the café, he returned to the underground, whose platforms displayed commuters like chess pieces on a board, only Artur was uncertain as to what strategies were at work.

On the train he felt walled in by other the passengers, sombre faces, expressions skewed into countless other expressions. A young woman offered him her seat, but he glanced away with a polite shake of the head.

He remembered the first time he'd travelled on the underground, pleasantly surprised on seeing the wide accommodating platforms, how clean it was. Eventually though it changed, became something less than had been intended. Maybe it was the day he saw the woman violently arguing with a ticket inspector, or the time the transport police stormed a train in full riot gear in response to a fight between Legia and Polonia football fans. He stared at his reflection in the window, an old man holding onto the overhead hand rail with slumped shoulders.

Early last year in February, Artur had been taking Zuzanna to the new Chopin museum. Two young men had sat across the train aisle from them, watching with bemused expressions. He'd managed to ignore them for most of the journey, only snapping when the smirking developed into stifled laughter.

"Show some respect you little bastards."

His wife, drowsy with medication, and startled awake, had presumed Artur was speaking to her. He might have wept if she hadn't called him by her father's name. Somehow it lessened the heartache.

This was the underground now, no different than anywhere else in the city, snaking beneath its many districts, through the darkness, each train ride given an abnormal musicality comprised of disdain and aggression.

On Saturday he shuffled into his daughter's apartment expecting to see his eight-year old granddaughter.

"Where's Maya?"

Ania took his coat, hung it up for him.

"She's having a sleepover at a friend's."

She led him like a child by the hand into a room full of strangers.

"HAPPY RETIREMENT," they roared at him, followed by the machine-gun sound of popping champagne corks.

Screwing his face into an expression bordering on gratitude, he wagged a conciliatory finger at Ania. Gregory, her husband, wagged one back.

"As if we'd let this go," he beamed.

Ania had assembled a collection of distant family and acquaintances, none of his real friends. Those who were still alive had either retired to the coast to live out their fears alone, or moved in with their own families in other cities.

After feigning an aversion to the champagne, Artur made his excuses to escape.

"I'm not drinking," Gregory said much too chirpily. "I can drive you if you really want to go?"

"I know you went to a lot of trouble on my behalf."

Ania made the appropriate sounds.

"You don't need me to have a good time," he said.

His daughter said goodbye at the door, making him feel guilty when she said he could sleep over.

"I prefer my own bed," he said, giving her a kiss on the cheek.

Outside his block, Gregory waved from the car, the light on the passenger side illuminating the interior. As Artur jangled his keys, blood seeped out of Gregory's mouth, staining his otherwise perfectly straight teeth.

Later that evening, Artur lay awake, staring at the gap between the curtains. He hated sleeping alone more than anything else. Most of his adult life Zuzanna had been right beside him, her body a comforting barrier during the uncertainty of sleepless nights.

It was still relatively early, young boisterous people passing below his fifth floor window, yelling, arguing, calling one another's names.

Before Zuzanna's death, Artur hadn't really noticed the noise so much. Now it intruded upon sleep with such regularity it was becoming part of his dreams.

*

He could have taken the bus since it was a long walk, but the champagne had yet to loosen its effect. Besides, the exercise would do him good.

Several streets from his block a taxi drew up to the kerb, letting out two women. They stretched into the night air, chatting about their evening adventures, before sauntering off in opposite directions. The smell of marijuana drifted after them, blood trailing the pavement where they'd been standing. A tram passed, windows like portraits with passengers' faces. From the steps of an underground station, a crowd rushed the changing of the lights. What was wrong with people these days?

Since his childhood Warsaw had gone through numerous transformations. Nothing had been as traumatic as the smouldering fires of the post-war years, streets and buildings reduced to apocalyptic rubble, only to be raised up once more in shining praise of a new regime. Artur would never forget running alongside his mother as they carted blocks of stone to a mill-yard, their efforts rewarded with a basket of mouldy bread. Such memories would always remain fixed in place.

In the late 70s, there had been a brief respite. Food in the shops, clothes to buy, people daringly wearing the same faces they wore in private, suspicious yet hopeful. A hint of change, of growing anticipation.

Then as the new decade arrived, a familiar stink had pervaded the shipyards; a return to disintegration. But as it spread out across the cities like so many times before, it had the opposite effect than of earlier, people suddenly galvanized into insurrection, animated against a system they no longer feared.

The faceless bureaucrats declared their dominance to be unassailable, pronouncing their official decrees with the same didactic certainty as always, as tanks like wheeled monoliths appeared on the streets. But as the masks stayed off, and as the voices grew, the dissent broadened, swelled, and finally swallowed up its opposition. And somehow, against the accepted narrative they'd been taught for so long, the indoctrinated truth, the slumbering contraption of Soviet rule simply shrivelled up, and was swept away without a backward glance. 1989, a good year, a promise of something new, that things would be different.

But as he turned into the street with the now defunct gas lamps, he realised promises were often the unrealised wishes of dreamers. And nowhere more was this evident than in the districts of the capital. This one in particular. This street in particular.

The electric street lights threw everything into ugly relief, especially a large house enclosed by a high wall. The gates were unlocked, as was its front door. Inside, a marble staircase ascended into a hallway of teak furniture, bloody handprints inking polished balustrades. A corpse lay slumped halfway up the stairs. Blood soaked clothes gave nothing away about their identity, age and sex indeterminate. In one of the upstairs bedrooms, he found it in a corner, watching the street with its many eyes, none of which were its own.

"Soon," it said, gesturing at the other houses.

NOT YET PLAYERS

The figure on the grassy hilltop resembled a scarecrow, its baggy head tilted to the earth, not the sky.

*

When they reached Chapel Hill the rain finally stopped, revealing a village of narrow winding streets, the sky a distant frown above smudged moorland. Jenny thought it was picturesque enough to make it onto one of the postcards framed in the post office window across from the car park.

"I'd loathe being a teenager growing up around these parts," she said.

Bill and Sophie were comparing their Google maps, checking street names. Andy was leaning against the car, smoking a cigarette.

"Thank God for the Internet," he said.

She couldn't tell if he was being serious, he had that kind of face, an at times unreadable demeanour.

In the post office window, a CLOSED sign hung in the door, adverts for miscellaneous items: bikes, children's toys, old fridges. One of the adverts made her look twice: *Hungry Celluloid TV Productions* searching for FUTURE STARS. Is that you? Call this number NOW: 76-53-8745.

"We're ready," Bill said, consulting his clipboard as if it contained the answers to all of the world's problems.

"You'd have thought the Internet would have phased out this kind of leg work by now," Andy complained.

Jenny had been thinking the exact same thing since head office had sent an e-mail instructing their team to conduct a door to door survey of Chapel Hill.

"In some respects, I can see why. We do get less responses when we e-mail people," Sophie said.

"Still doesn't explain the sudden change in data collection. And what's so special about this place anyway?"

"Lorraine Rogers from logistics chose it. Apparently she grew up here," Sophie said.

"She's been acting strange lately," Andy replied.

"How do you mean?"

"Just weird."

Bill folded his arms, his team leader countenance resumed with an exaggerated cough.

"Let's get a move on shall we?"

The four of them walked to the end of the street, a scattering of bungalows and rain soaked trees.

"Give me a call once you're finished." Bill tucked his clipboard under one arm, before pointing Sophie toward a cul-de-sac.

Jenny walked up the driveway to a large house.

"Are you from the TV?"

A woman in a pink fleecy nightgown stood on the front doorstep, grey hair swamped with rollers. She reminded Jenny of a character from a comedy show her grandmother used to watch years before.

"Hi there. Yes, I am."

The woman shouted into the house.

"Didn't I tell you they'd be calling round?"

A male voice shouted back.

"Who's that then?"

The woman shook her head.

"He's the original doubting Thomas, that one. I said to him they were looking for extras."

"Extras?"

"Isn't that what they call them?"

Jenny recalled the advert in the post office window.

"I'm sorry. I should have made myself clear. I'm collecting statistical data. You must be..." Jenny looked at her list, pinpointing the name next to the address, "Mrs Harper?"

The woman adjusted one of the rollers in her hair, nodding disappointedly.

Jenny couldn't quite reconcile the cheap pink nightgown to the house. Mrs Harper stood aside, letting Jenny see the hallway. Was she inviting her inside?

"A cup of tea?" she asked, eyes darting across the street to where Andy stood talking to a man in a garden. "I've put the kettle on."

"That's very kind, only I'm afraid I really don't have the time."

She must have caught Mrs Harper in the middle of doing her makeup, eyeliner or mascara smudging her left cheek.

"Are you absolutely sure I can't tempt you?" she asked, opening the door a fraction wider.

*

The player, who was acting as a housewife, closed the door on the woman who wasn't yet a player.

"And cut!"

From a cupboard beneath the stairs the Director instructed the DOP to move the camera back into position.

"Get her before she's out of shot."

The DOP shifted the camera to the living room window as the young woman walked down the driveway and out of sight.

The actress playing Mrs Harper tore off the wig she'd been wearing.

"Good work, Marge," the Director said.

She blushed. The acting parts were stacking up, soon she'd have a CV the envy of everyone in the village.

"Do me a favour, take care of Faye," the Director instructed.

The real Mrs Harper, *Faye*, lay face down on a pile of large plastic black bin bags on the upstairs landing.

"Can I chop her up?" she asked, looking at the Director, his face swimming out of focus.

"Knock yourself out."

Upstairs, Mr Harper was in the master bedroom, a blood soaked hatchet in his hands.

"It's funny, you know."

"What is Ted?"

He gazed at the hatchet.

"How much this looks like real blood."

*

Jenny held out her list to Andy.

"That's the last twelve."

Andy compared her list to his own.

"Same here."

"What's this local based reality show everyone's hooked on? It's not listed with the other programmes."

"I'll call Bill."

She waited while he dialled.

"No answer. What now?"

"I say we do one more street. If it comes up again, we'll call it quits. Tell Bill we did our best. He hates anomalies. It'll freak him out."

*

"I can't believe you haven't seen Tales of Gruesomeness," the teenage girl said, rolling chewing gum round her mouth.

Jenny stood in the doorway of a detached house, its front garden containing more litter than the pavement. A woman in cut-off denim shorts and a stained blouse flung the door open, dragging her daughter to one side.

"It's on now if you want to have a look."

A TV blared from behind a door, the hallway unnaturally bright, as if lit by powerful lights.

"No thank you, Mrs. Preston. I've got a few more houses to get through."

That was a lie. There was no point Jenny telling her she could easily predict each interview by now.

"You're missing out," the mother said.

"Maybe next time," Jenny replied, not quite knowing what she was promising or why she'd even said it in the first place. The woman exuded a physically awkward presence, as if her clothes belonged on somebody else. Jenny was expecting her to denounce the scene on the doorstep as hackneyed.

Hurrying to join Andy, the sun diminished above the hills, spreading shadows across the village.

"Any luck?"

Andy stood waiting for her on the corner of the street.

"Nothing from either of them."

Jenny pointed to a pub on the other side of the road.

"We're officially allowed a lunch break."

"That's the answer I was hoping for. Lead on."

The only people in the pub were a gropup of elderly men in an alcove.

"What can I get you?" the barman asked.

"Bitter," she said, and gesturing to Andy who was slotting money into a bandit machine. "And a pint of Kronenbourg."

Jenny brought the drinks to the table by a window. Andy sat down, took a gulp. Wiping his mouth, he scanned the pub.

"Win anything?"

"Nope. Never do."

Jenny glanced around the pub.

"Look," she said.

Andy followed her gaze towards the elderly men. Everyone was watching a TV set above the bar. The screen filled with blood as a knife plunged into an unseen victim screaming off camera.

Jenny shouted over to the men.

"*Tales of Gruesomeness*?"

One of the men nodded, his attention never leaving the screen.

"Charming."

They finished their pints and as they were leaving, they spotted Bill and Sophie walking towards them.

"Here they are at last," Andy called.

"Something's up with Sophie."

Bill had one arm locked about her waist, pulling her closer than she seemed comfortable with. They'd been dating for six months, and there were rumours Bill was going to propose her to any day soon. Sophie's makeup had run down her cheeks, black smudges beneath her eyes.

"She's been crying," Jenny said.

Bill let go of Sophie, and stepping forward, swung his right arm at Andy.

"That's for you," he said.

Jenny didn't react, not immediately. This was a game, a sick joke, something the three of them had dreamt up to scare her.

"Andy?"

He remained pinned inside the trajectory of the arc Bill had flung at him. When he did finally move, his head lowered, slowly, eyes becoming unfocused, blood welling up beneath his shirt. Bill stepped back as if into position, a knife in his hand. Jenny grabbed Andy as he slipped, stumbling, blood pooling about his feet.

Sophie laughed.

"Do it again," she urged.

"No, wait," Jenny screamed.

The knife jabbed into Andy's left cheek, cutting down in a jagged bloody line towards his mouth.

Jenny let go of her colleague, knowing she was next if she didn't run.

*

She drove Bill's car as fast as she could, tearing around hairpin bends like a heroine in an action movie. It was a miracle she didn't hit any traffic coming the other way or skid off the road into a tree. It might have seemed coincidental the keys being left in the ignition like that, but she was operating on panic. The sun sailed by, playing shadow games behind rain clouds.

"And cut!" someone yelled from afar.

Jenny pumped the accelerator, screaming at the top of her voice, the car shuddering to a stop beside the road. Out of the driver's window she watched as people came streaming down the hillside towards her.

The villagers stood beneath a tree, the upper boughs displaying a dozen corpses on ropes.

"This is almost the end," the Director said.

The more Jenny looked at him, the more insubstantial he became. Smoke drifted away from his face, black tendrils caught on a breeze. The corpses blew back and forth, reanimated by the suddenly changing season.

"Is that me?" Jenny asked, meaning the mangled effigy on the wooden cross jutting out of the earth.

"Naturally."

"It can't be."

The villagers laughed.

"Why not?"

"This is just a story. I refuse to believe in it. I refuse to believe in you."

"Believe in this," he said, removing the cowl from the scarecrow's face.

AMONG FLAMES, DARKNESS

At eight-thirty every morning, Alice arrives for her shift. A woman of contagious jollity, she's so much more than the name on the badge pinned to the lapel of her uniform. Despite being a single parent with three teenage children and putting in long hours, she fusses over me as if I were part of her family, too.

"It's bit nippy out today," she says.

She's nothing at all like the other care workers, those whose shrill voices are more robotic than the talking clock.

"I'll turn over the one in the box room," Alice yells down the stairs.

I haven't had a guest in years, yet she always prepares the spare bedroom just in case. A tidy beacon of hope in a landscape of dead friends and unwanted memories. Her shifts rotate with three other care workers, all of whom are monstrously dull people. None of them come close to Alice, neither sharing her devotion, or more importantly, her kindness.

"She's more likely to kiss arse than clean one," I once heard them describe her, a lie to cover their own inadequacies. I pay an agency for their services from my dwindling savings. Hopefully, this won't stretch the entire bank balance of my life.

The worst of these women is Janet Petrie. She refers to her shift as penance for crimes committed in a past life. She has particular loathing for anyone she believes has outdone her in some way. People like Alice. People like me. There's no reason for her hatred, nothing that makes sense. She's just programmed that way.

Alice yells from upstairs.

"Shall I bring down one of your talking books?"

"Yes, please."

"Which one?"

"Them Robert Ludlum ones."

Alice appears, eyes lit up, smiling. The audio book was a Christmas present from her last year. How nice that something so small should make someone so happy.

*

I don't hear Petrie enter the house, the audio book on full volume. I smell her perfume first, the one which smells of fruit.

Rotten apples.

"Like a burglar, you are. More stealth than common sense. Ring the bell next time."

"I do. You never hear."

We have this conversation every week. Petrie thinks I might be showing signs of dementia. Truth is, I repeat myself because it drives her crazy.

She goes upstairs to run my evening bath. She hates this task more than anything else, and strains to manoeuvre my bulk into the chair-lift. She hurriedly unpeels my pyjamas, managing to get me into the bath, before retreating downstairs to have a cigarette in the garden. I lie in the tepid water, gripping the safety rails, wondering about the FOR SALE sign in the overgrown front garden of number thirty-three. It recently appeared without warning.

That house sticks out as much as my Georgian property does. Both conspicuous are minor landmarks, fading anomalies in their surroundings. In a way, it's a comfort to know I'm not the only survivor in my neighbourhood.

After only ten minutes, Petrie shouts up the stairs, the disdain in her voice impossible to ignore.

"Do you want me to come get you?"

I stare at the liver spots on my frail bony hands.

"Well, if you don't do it, I'll be here until tomorrow morning, won't I?"

"Cheeky bastard," she mutters, thinking my hearing is going the way of my mind.

"Leave me a bit longer," I reply.

*

It was the second night of blackouts, the entire neighbourhood buried in quivering darkness. German bombers had thrown the city into primordial existence, electricity snuffed out, only not for pterodactyls, but for planes carrying payloads. The streets were unfamiliar without lights, bombed out houses exposed as jagged outlines against the shifting sky. A high-pitched shriek sliced the air, an air-raid warden blowing his whistle.

"Hurry your feet, lad," my father said, leading us into a warren of streets. His voice was the rumble of the German bombers heard from a distance, waiting for an opportunity to terrify.

"I can hear 'em," I said.

He grabbed hold of my earlobe and twisted it between his thumb and forefinger.

"How many times have I told you? Them. Them. Not 'em. Your mother mightn't care about these things. However, I do," he said.

He let go with what felt like reluctance. My ear stung, but not wanting to give him the satisfaction, I refused to let him see how much it hurt.

Last week at the Playhouse, the other local kids had been shouting at the matinee film in a frenzy of grammatically incorrect glee, nobody there to reprimand them about their frequent use of inaccurate language.

"Go get 'em Nazi cockroaches," they'd sung together, as Robert Mills had gone in search of the enemy in *Old Bill and Sons.*

"I tell you, I won't have you speaking like those idiots' children."

He believed my occasional lapses justified his treatment of me. It was nothing compared to how he behaved towards my mother. I often heard him accuse her *of laying down with just about everybody in the vicinity of our front doorstep and coming home speaking like them*. I couldn't quite equate him to the personality my mother described from their early courting days. If such a person had ever existed, he was more an accomplished form propaganda than anything Lord Haw Haw broadcast.

"That place is a waste of money and time. Probably a blessing in disguise what happened to it."

A German bomb had destroyed the Playhouse the previous evening, the explosion having upturned the pavements in the surrounding streets, stone slabs littering the ground like discarded monoliths.

"You should have left me where I was," my father said.

My mother had sent me to fetch him from Archibald's motorcycle repair shop, by night an illicit brewery den. My father made no pretence why he went there.

Ralph Worley came out of a side street, stopping us with a blast on his whistle.

"Hurry on home with your boy there."

The air raid warden slunk back into the darkness with such indifference he was either a phantom or unaware of his own presence at times.

"Has a finger in every meat pie this side of the river," my father said, referring to rumours about Worley's black market dealings.

We continued walking past houses that were poor relations to the buildings they'd once been, naked rafters poking up at the night sky. Suddenly, the air-raid siren wailed to life.

I had heard the sound plenty of times before this evening, but only from the safety of our house. My mother would be out of her mind with worry, crouching down inside the air-raid shelter, intoning her prayers and rattling her rosary, whichever came first. I hoped our neighbour Mrs McGowan was with her, even if she had a habit of sticking her head out of the door during the middle of an air-raid, sceptical of the German's ability to hit us.

I wanted to tell my father I was frightened, but the large head on those intimidating shoulders turned its neck as if searching the streets for some half remembered short-cut. I knew when to stay quiet. The siren abruptly stopped. My fear mushroomed into something far worse.

I felt it in the air first, long before I saw anything. A sense of weight descending, sucking up the air, filling the pitch black sky with pressure. Not more than half a mile away a huge explosion ripped through the city centre, pulling apart rooftops as if they were mere inconveniences.

We ran towards what I hoped was our street, but it was difficult to say in the blackness of our rapidly disintegrating world. Behind us black smoke spiralled above factory towers, blocking out the horizon, spreading out.

In the light of the explosion my father wore an alien expression. I couldn't say whether it was terror or defiance. Even if he'd been young enough to fight in the war, he wouldn't have gone. Not willingly. Not after Ypres. Like most men of his generation, he rarely talked about his experiences. I'd once made the mistake of asking him. He'd been drinking most of the day, slouched over the kitchen table, spooning pea soup into his stubbly mouth, struggling to sober up. My mother had almost succeeded in manoeuvring me out of the kitchen, before my father looked up, realising what was going on.

"Leave him, let him stay," he said, pushing the bowl of soup to one side. He pointed to the chair opposite. "Sit down."

I did as I was told.

"So, you'd like to hear a story, would you?"

I was too afraid to say I'd changed my mind. He wasn't wearing his spectacles, eyes bleary with excess. On the cusp of exploding, anything could set him off. As his audience my sole duty was to remain silent. I listened as he slogged through muddy fields in leaking boots, or dug out dead comrades from collapsed trenches. I listened as he crawled through a pockmarked landscape in which the cannons never ceased their barrage, pounding the world into bone dust. I listened knowing this would haunt my sleep for weeks to come. But what I remembered most was the look on his face as he was telling me. The same one he had now.

"As slow as your mother is at doing what's best for her," my father yelled, pulling on my arm like a recalcitrant child.

Flames spread across the city; fierce colours. Such was the noise, I felt I only had to turn the corner to see where the bombs had landed. The world was burning to the ground, being reduced to a smouldering carcass. The image of a bomb hitting our house and blowing my mother into a thousand irretrievable pieces made me hurry after my father. He grabbed my hand, his panic as keenly felt as the elevated thrum of my own heart. I looked up to see the stars had been blacked out by a tide of monstrous droning planes, bulging fortresses.

Another broiling sun lit up the neighbourhood, only this one made tinder of the trees in the next street over. My father staggered along the pavement, looking from left to right amongst the hedgerows as if desperate to locate somebody. He was no longer the same man who stalked our house as the minotaur had its labyrinth, but was knee deep in the very worst his imagination could offer.

"In here," he shouted, releasing my hand.

There was a house in our street much older than any other building within the vicinity. It had been built in the Regency period, a squat stone villa that had once served as lodgings for workers on a now vanished estate. There were all kinds of rumours about the occupants, about their late night parties, of delivery men coming and going all hours. And it was here my father was heading.

"We can't leave mother," I shouted.

He struck me without even breaking stride. I instantly tasted blood. I didn't care, there was worse pain waiting for me if we stayed outside for much longer. We needed somewhere to hide.

I followed him as he lumbered around side of the house, his shadow a wavering threat not to pursue him.

I found him in the garden banging on an air-raid shelter, yelling to be let inside. The garden swam with heat. The air-raid shelter door opened. There was lull in the bombing, silence except for the crackling of flames. My father gesticulated with whoever was in the doorway, shoulders raised.

"Is it just you?" someone asked.

My father muttered something, before pushing past them. Was he intending to leave me behind in the middle of a bombing raid?

"There's another one out here...quick, lad."

The door didn't shut, not yet. I ran, bending down to accommodate the height of the shelter, squinting as someone thrust an oil lamp into my face.

"Just a boy," I heard somebody say.

"Close the door," a voice declared from the furthermost reaches of the shelter.

"Do as the man says," my father barked at me.

There was no trace of shame on his face, only exhaustion. He sat on the floor with his back against the curving shelter wall.

The old man lowered the oil lamp.

"A full house tonight," he said.

Two other elderly male faces came bobbing out of the darkness.

"A father and son," one of them said.

All three were wearing the exact same black suits, high stiff collars, polished black buttons on the cuffs, wide neat lapels. They looked as if they'd come straight from an evening out at Holliston theatre.

"My cousins," the old man said, waving the gas lamp.

The other two were sitting on a long wooden bench much lower down than the rest of the shelter. The roof sloped over their heads, ending at a wall of loosely assembled bricks.

The old man saw me looking.

"Tumuli throw up all sort of folk, don't they?"

His cousins tipped me a wink, either amused by our dramatic entry or the confusion on my face.

"Thank you for letting us share your shelter," my father said.

"I know you," the old man said.

My father directed his gaze at the ceiling.

"It seems everybody knows everybody around here."

Undeterred, the old man continued.

"It's the house at the end of the row if I'm not mistaken?"

One of the others inclined his head towards the rear of the shelter as if wanting me to follow his gaze.

"For once boy, will you pay attention?" my father said, a vein pulsing in his forehead.

The old man smiled at me, waiting for an introduction.

"Peter Constable, sir."

"I'm not Lord Muck of the manor. Just Jim will do."

Something caught my eye. Were the impact of the bombs making the shadows move at the other end of the shelter?

"Didn't you used to work at the Morning Chronicle?" Jim asked.

My father nodded, but didn't wish to elaborate.

"And you?" he asked the old man.

I could smell my father's sour whiskey breath in the confined space.

"Retired, but still busy."

I listened to their voices, which sounded so very far away even in the confined space of the shelter. My body felt suddenly very clammy. I put out a hand to steady myself, fingers grasping at nothing. Before I could do anything I was on the floor and blinking back the darkness, staring up at Jim. I felt reluctant hands on my collars, pulling me up. The broken capillaries in my father's nose shone in the light.

"I can hardly breathe," he said, this being his only allowance I wasn't at fault.

The air in the shelter smelled like damp earth. It was as if we were somewhere else, further below ground.

"You a bit worse for wear there, lad?" Jim asked.

"It happens a lot," my father said.

"I dare say it does."

Somewhere in the city a bomb exploded, shaking the air-raid shelter, wooden supports raining earth.

"I'm fine," I replied, realising my mistake before I could say anything to correct my lack of formality.

It was an impossible instinct for my father to ignore. He took my ear, twisted it much harder than earlier.

"Enough of that, he's not your wife," said Jim, pulling my father away.

"I'll say when enough is enough."

My father shrugged off the old man.

"He's not even mine."

Outside a bomb struck our street, the ground heaving with oceanic proportions, upending everyone in the shelter. Pitched into suffocating blackness, I heard my father cry out. Something inside the shelter collapsed, bricks tumbling to the ground. A blast of cold air hit my face, followed by a nauseating stench. I was on my knees when something slithered past me. It touched my foot and recoiled away, searching for someone else.

"Don't worry, lad. He'll go down a treat," someone said.

I didn't wait to hear beyond the punch line and pulled the door open, clambering out into the garden. The air tasted of smoke, the horizon filled with flames. I was halfway across the garden when I heard a thunderous satisfying belch. Despite having sustained a hatred him for my father every literal second of my boyhood, I now prayed for him.

*

The next morning a group of air-raid wardens discovered me wandering among the rubble of the neighbourhood.

"Must have been out all night," one of them said, stooping down to wrap his jacket around my trembling shoulders. He smelled of smoke, soot ingrained into his face as if he was a portrait etching of himself.

The warders presumed I'd become separated from my father, and took it in turns to admire my resilience, religiously intoning their astonishment.

"Nothing short of a miracle."

"God was looking down on you last night, son."

"Must be blessed."

They escorted me home, trumpeting my arrival to anyone they met on the way. For these men, careworn and exhausted, with their fire blackened faces, I was proof prayers were sometimes acknowledged.

When we reached my street everyone cheered, clapping me on the back, ruffling my hair. One warder put me up on his shoulders, carrying me past the charred remains of my neighbours' houses. My own house still stood, as did number thirty-three, somehow having avoided what the rest hadn't.

My father's body was never recovered and I let my mother believe what remained of him was somewhere out among the ruins of our bombed out city. I'd told her he'd panicked and run off without thinking, out of his mind with terror, screaming nonsense at the top of his voice.

"Maybe it was Ypres?" she wondered aloud.

"I think it must have been," I replied, hating myself for lying to her. But it was better than having to relive what had happened in the air-raid shelter.

"No excuse leaving you like that," she replied, before adding, "perhaps it's best it ended this way."

*

I've convinced Petrie to take me outside so we can look for an imaginary cat.

"What cat?" she asks, wondering if my hypothetical dementia has kicked in.

I explain, and as she listens she's unable to suppress her obvious delight at what I tell her.

"Poor little thing."

I lie, claiming Alice had recently given me a kitten to keep me company, only it had escaped out the back door. Petrie can't believe her luck, a breach of company policy. Carers aren't allowed to give pets.

Eager to land Alice in trouble, she doesn't even think to look for evidence of a litter tray or tins of cat food, so determined in pursuit of her perceived life enemy.

"That's the garden she went into. It was definitely her I saw," I say, pointing to number thirty-three.

Petrie leaves me in the wheelchair in front of the house and walks into the garden, which is a jungle of disuse.

"Are you sure?"

"The little thing's probably found the old air-raid shelter they've still got back there."

Petrie disappears round the corner in search of the cat. I know the air-raid shelter still exists, just as I also know the loosely boarded up doorway has a gap just about big enough to let somebody inside.

"I've found it!" Petrie shouts.

"Make sure you look inside."

Her voice rises for a second or two, before being cut off mid-sentence.

"Petrie?"

Silence.

"Petrie?"

I give it ten more minutes, and then wheel myself back to the house. I operate the ramp access and enter. I manage to pour myself a gin, and even have a cigarette from the pack left on the kitchen sideboard. When I'm ready, I'll ring Alice and tell her all about the good news.

THE EXTRA

During a production of *Rigoletto* at the Theatre Wielki Narodowa, Rafał noticed one of the extras slinking across stage, seemingly trying to extricate themselves from the rest of the cast without being noticed. The woman wore a narrow black gown, and a lacy black veil covered her face. Having no idea what was happening in the story, and bored out of his mind, he pointed her out to Hania.

"Where's she off to?"

His girlfriend hushed him in an even louder voice.

Rafał had never been to the opera before, this being a birthday gift from Hania. His idea of music was Earl Hines and Johnny Hodges, not people in period costumes blasting unfathomable songs at excruciating levels at one another. By the third act, he knew his relationship with Hania wouldn't last the weekend. While a month wasn't long, as far as he was concerned they would always be strangers in the making. Hania was constantly referring to his cultural development, which was about as insulting as he could imagine coming from any person.

The woman glided across stage, Rafał craning his neck to see where she was going. She was like a hesitant party-goer, juggling uncertainty about their role.

"Are you bored?"

Hania gripped the balcony rail.

"Don't do it," he joked.

She pulled her face.

"It cost a lot for these tickets, and you're just sitting here looking off into space."

"I'm not."

"It's so annoying when you do things like this."

He stood up without really considering what he was doing.

"Where are you going?"

He squeezed past the other audience members, already wondering if Hania was going to come after him. In the lift, he imagined her running down the stairs, aiming to ambush him in the foyer. By the time he was standing in the street flagging down a taxi, his escape remained unimpeded. When he got back to his block, he rang Bartek.

"I thought you were at the opera no less," his friend teased.

"I was, and now I'm not. I'll fill you in when I see you. So, what's the plan?"

"I was going to say you're welcome to join me at a party in Bielany. But I don't think Hania would like this type of crowd."

"Don't worry, she won't be coming. We split up."

"When did that happen?"

"About thirty minutes ago."

"Who did the dumping?"

"Me."

"Harsh."

"You think?"

"Get your arse over here."

"I need to change first. I'll be there as soon as I can" he said, referring to the suit Hania had told to wear to the opera.

In the foyer of his block by the individual post boxes, a woman was peering at the community information board. He didn't pay much attention to her as the lift arrived, only that she was dressed from head to toe in black.

In his bedroom, he changed into a pair of denim jeans and a pullover, no longer feeling like the impostor Hania had been attempting to create out of him. Rafał understood why none of his friends had ever liked her. She wasn't easy to warm to. He recalled her criticizing his collection of jazz records. *It's a bit erratic, like they're just making stuff up as they go along. I think Miles Davies is overrated.*

The party was at a house opposite the Bielany practice airfield, where a single engine plane was towing a glider behind it. Before he pressed the doorbell, he watched as the wooden plane curved up through the sky after the more powerful yet less graceful version. As the planes rose higher, a figure appeared far away alongside the perimeter fence, their black featureless body only identifiable by a pale, insubstantial blur of a face.

A young woman greeted him at the door.

"Who are you?"

Bartek came running over, putting an arm around the woman's shoulder. She slipped out from under his sizeable weight.

"He's a friend of mine," Bartek said.

"I didn't think you had any."

"Aren't we friends?"

"In your dreams," she said, before escaping to her friends in another room.

"She's nobody's fool that one," Bartek said.

"I can see," Rafał replied.

They went from room to room, a trajectory practiced plenty of times before, doing what they could to enter into conversations. Nobody was interested, perhaps sensing their intentions. Many of the women made Rafał him feel less sure of what he saying, or even why he was saying it.

In the garden he lit up a cigarette, the Bielany airfield stretching out in front of the house. In the fading light, he saw there were other smokers, chatting to one another, but ignoring him. A woman stood by the fence, and as a light flickered on in the house, it illuminated her black clothes.

He smoked his cigarette and watched a glider fly over the neighbouring rooftops. He glanced at the woman, her face turned away from him. There was no point in approaching her since it was obvious she wanted to be left alone.

He found Bartek in the kitchen telling jokes to a group of women, the punch line so sexist he failed to raise even a groan of disappointment. Rafał was at least aware of his shortcomings, whereas Bartek had the kind of preconceptions about women he'd been carrying around with him since a teenager.

"You're hard to please," Bartek said, straying out into the corridor, searching for someone not yet familiar with his charmless idiocy.

One of the women shook her head as she passed Rafal. This would be his best opportunity to *apologise for his friend's inappropriate sense of humour*. Before he could say anything, the woman gave him a look which demolished any ideas he might have been harbouring about talking to her.

He went looking for Bartek again, this time to tell him he was going home. This party had been a mistake and he was starting to regret being so hasty with Hania. Had his reaction really been justified?

He found his friend in the garden with the woman he'd seen earlier, Bartek's pudgy arms encircling her slender waist, her face obscured by his.

"Hey, I'm heading home."

There was no response from Bartek. The woman tightened her arms about his neck, pulling him closer, her black clothes absorbing him. There was an audible smacking of lips, and Bartek's back leg twitched.

"I'll leave you to it," Rafal said raising his voice.

Bartek's head jerked back slightly, as if he might finally acknowledge Rafal, but the woman's hands clasped the nape of his neck and pulled him towards her so closely it didn't seem physically possible to do so.

"Right, see you later."

Rafal left the party feeling guilty for begrudging his friend the same kind of attention he was himself also so desperate for. He had no right to expect anything from anyone, especially after walking out on Hania. No matter how rude she might have been to him, which didn't seem so bad the more he thought about it, nobody deserved to be treated that way.

The walk back to his block wasn't far, but it felt much longer than it should have done. It was because of the security guard pacing the other side of the fence separating the Bielany airfield from the road. It was too dark to see him clearly, but every so often he'd put on a spurt of speed as if wanting to catch up with Rafal. Not until he turned the corner into his own neighbourhood did he stop worrying the guard was following him.

On his street he saw somebody outside the church on the Wólczynska intersection. The harder he stared the more they began to resemble a cluster of shadows merging, before he decided that was what it had to be.

As the lift clattered down into the foyer somebody walked into the block behind him. There was a giggle. He shouldn't look, it was obviously a drunk neighbour trying to get his attention. The lift appeared, and Rafał glanced sideways. It was the woman Bartek had been with when he'd left the party, her clothes somehow a denser black under the foyer lights. So, somebody had been following him after all.

He waited for Bartek to show in the entrance doorway, thinking this had to be a practical joke. The woman slightly turned her head so that she came into profile, but whatever she had over her face meant he saw only the tremulous flutter of the fabric as she was breathing.

She shuffled a side-step, away from the entrance, following the line of the wall, her gown running along the floor, a sound very much like hands itching.

Rafał grabbed the lift door, and thought about saying something about Bartek and his taste in women, but didn't want to admit that he was jealous of his friend.

The woman turned one corner so that she was moving along the wall containing the post boxes. He could hear her breathing, a resonant exhalation, feet scraping at the concrete floor as she kept up that odd slanting, shambling walk.

He felt a twinge of anger that Bartek wasn't going to show his face and admit the joke was no longer so funny, and Rafal opened the lift door. As he pressed the button, a shadow coloured the window, darkening the interior. The woman stood on the other side of the glass panel, her head bowed, one head reaching for the handle, the cloth over her face flapping gently.

"Tell Bartek he's hilarious."

He drank some water before he got in bed and fell asleep, only to be woken by a sound in the living room. It must have been a neighbour upstair. He got up to make sure, peering into the living room, switching on the light at the same time. Except it didn't work. This didn't prevent him from seeing that there here was somebody standing in the corner by the balcony door.

Bartek.

Rafał must have left the door unlocked. Did his friend really think this was funny? He walked across the living room and grabbed his friend by the shoulder.

"Pack it in," he said.

It wasn't Bartek. Rafał was glad the light hadn't worked, for as his hand slid off the woman's shoulder there was something wrong about the feel of her body beneath the material of her gown, the way her skin squelched.

"Come out, Bartek. This stopped being funny ages ago."

The woman giggled like before in the foyer, a sound so truly awful in the darkness of his apartment that he shuddered when she lifted her hands, both of which were dripping with blackness.

"Come closer," she said.

The last thing he wanted was to get any nearer, only he wasn't going to let her frighten him in his own home.

He seized her hands, pulling them away from her face. The silky black material of her gown, the frilly cuffs of her sleeves, sucked at his fingers as if wanting to absorb every last drop of him. He heard her exhaling again as in the foyer, the sound much more amplified.

"Oh, I'm going to come closer," he said.

Rafał ripped the veil off the woman's head, expecting to hear her protests before he saw her face.

She smiled at him instead, her mouth the only feature in that shining hairless dome. He couldn't look away from the mouth, not even when she threw her arms about him and pinned him to her body, which began to open like one large impossible wound.

"Let me taste your disbelief," she said.

BIBLIOGRAPHY

Permanent Hunger – The Signal Block and Other Tales (2012 / Gallows Press).

A Greater Horror – Dark Valentine Magazine (2005), Unknown Causes (2014 / Gallows Press).

Appearances – The Signal Block and Other Tales (2012 / Gallows Press).

The Seat – Here & Now (2005), Unknown Causes (2014 / Gallows Press).

The Places – Unknown Causes (2014 / Gallows Press).

And When The Lights Came On – The Signal Block and Other Tales (2012 / Gallows Press).

Not Yet Players – The Signal Block and Other Tales (2012 / Gallows Press).

Among Flames, Darkness – Unknown Causes (2014 / Gallows Press).

The Extra – Hungry Celluloid (2015 / Dark Minds Press).

BIOGRAPHY

Frank Duffy is the author of three short story collections, *The Signal Block & Other Tales*, *Unknown Causes*, and *Hungry Celluloid*. A single volume of his novelettes was published under the title *Mountains of Smoke*, comprised of the eponymous tale, 'Ambiguous', and 'Not Yet The End of The Story'. He grew up in Rainford, a provincial village in the north west of England, but now lives in Poland with his wife Angelika and dog, Mr Mole.

ADRIAN BALDWIN (COVER ARTIST)

Adrian is a Mancunian now living and working in Wales. Back in the 1990s, he wrote for various TV shows/personalities: Smith & Jones, Clive Anderson, Brian Conley, Paul McKenna, Hale & Pace, Rory Bremner (and a few others). Wooo, get him! Since then, he has written three screenplays—one of which received generous financial backing from the Film Agency for Wales. Then along came the global recession which kicked the UK Film industry in the nuts. What a bummer! Not to be outdone, he turned to novel writing—which had always been his real dream—and, in particular, a genre he feels is often overlooked; a genre he has always been a fan of: Dark Comedy (sometimes referred to as Horror's weird cousin). *Barnacle Brat* (a dark comedy for grown-ups), his first novel won Indie Novel of the Year 2016 award; his second novel *Stanley Mccloud Must Die!* (more dark comedy for grown-ups) published in 2016 and his third: *The Snowman And The Scarecrow* (another dark comedy for grown-ups) published in 2018. Adrian Baldwin has also written and published a number of dark comedy short stories. He designs book covers too—not just for his own books but for a growing number of publishers. For more information on the award-winning author, check out: https://adrianbaldwin.info/

DEMAIN PUBLISHING

To keep up to-date on all news DEMAIN (including future submission calls and releases) you can follow us in a number of ways:

BLOG:
www.demainpublishingblog.weebly.com

TWITTER:
@DemainPubUk

FACEBOOK PAGE:
Demain Publishing

INSTAGRAM:
Demainpublishing

Printed in Great Britain
by Amazon

51469917R00098